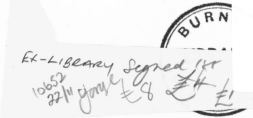
For the Clayesmore School Library

At the request of
Mallay Charters
Wolverton House 1982-83

Samuel Charters

£2
r 1st edn.
Signed Author

MR. JABI
AND
MR. SMYTHE

Also by Samuel Charters

Poetry
The Children
The Landscape at Bolinas
Heroes of the Prize Ring
Days
To this Place
From a London Notebook
From a Swedish Notebook
In Lagos
Of Those Who Died

Criticism
Some Poems/Poets

Biography, with Ann Charters
I Love (The story of Vladimir Mayakovsky and Lili Brik)

Translations
Baltics (from the Swedish of Tomas Tranströmer)
We Women (from the Swedish of Edith Södergran)

Music
Jazz: New Orleans
The Country Blues
Jazz: The New York Scene
The Poetry of the Blues
The Bluesmen
Robert Johnson
The Legacy of the Blues
Sweet as the Showers of Rain
The Swedish Fiddlers
Roots of the Blues: An African Search

MR. JABI
AND
MR. SMYTHE

a novel by
SAMUEL CHARTERS

Marion Boyars
New York. London

Published in the U.S.A. and Great Britain in 1983 by
MARION BOYARS PUBLISHERS
457 Broome Street, New York, N.Y. 10013
and
18 Brewer Street, London W1R 4AS.

Australian and New Zealand distribution by
Thomas C. Lothian Pty.
4-12 Tattersalls Lane, Melbourne, Victoria 3000.

Library of Congress Cataloguing in Publication Data
Charters, Samuel Barclay.
    Mr. Jabi and Mr. Smythe.
    I. Title.
PS3553.H327M7   1982   813'.54   82-12818

British Library Cataloguing in Publication Data
Charters, Samuel
    Mr. Jabi and Mr. Smythe.
    I. Title
    813'.54[F]   PS3553.H/
    ISBN 0-7145-2779-3 Cloth

Manufactured in the United States
Distributed in the United States by
The Scribner Book Companies, Inc.

for Annie

1.

Mr. Jabi always woke to the same sounds. The sounds of the birds shaking themselves loose from the night's shadows, the thudding noise of the women pounding millet for the morning's breakfast, the bleating of the goats, the clanking of the cattle as they were driven out to graze in the brush, children's laughter, men's loud calling drifting over the sagging fences of the village. The sounds made their way into his bare room, through the discolored mosquito netting that swathed the bed. After so many years they had become woven into the fabric of the netting, wound into its yellowing folds.

He always woke alone. Even when his wife shared his bed she was always gone before morning, busy in her part of the house. When he was not away on a trip he always woke up in the same room, always with the same oblong of light on the elongated piece of scuffed linoleum that was laid on the floor. The light that the morning sun spread across the space beside his bed had been part of his surroundings for so long that he would have noticed it only if its position had changed – if it weren't there for him to stretch his bare feet outward, as

7

he did every morning when he pushed himself out of the sagging bed, pulled the mosquito net open and stretched his arms over his head.

Outside the window there was the dry rustle of the chickens, the barking of the village dogs. Women chattered to each other as they clattered pans and broke sticks for fires. The air was a coarse texture of sounds filtering through the morning's golden sheen of light. Usually he heard the sounds as little as he noticed the objects around him in the room. They were part of the presence of the morning, something that he stretched his arms into, just as he stretched his feet out into the patch of sunlight on the floor. Like the sunlight, he would have noticed the sounds only if they weren't there.

But this morning as he woke and put his feet on the floor beside the bed he sat for a moment on the creaking mattress and looked around him. Across from him, on the plaster wall that he had haphazardly whitewashed whenever there was a little extra money, he could see the curling photographs that had hung there since he was new to the village and he had first moved into the house. Could his wife have been so young? There in the photograph they'd had taken just after their marriage she stood stiffly beside him, both of their faces shining with their nervousness. It was possible to follow their lives from one year to the next just by looking at the photographs. Mr. Jabi stood up, put on slippers and went over to the small collection dangling against the wall in crude frames taped together out of cardboard and painted window glass. There, along with the photographs of their children, with the photographs of himself in his first suit, with his first class as a young school teacher, beside the photographs of his wife and her family, were the photographs of Mr. Smythe.

The old snapshots had faded, but the faces were still clear. His face, so dark, and Mr. Smythe's face, so white. At first Mr. Smythe's was the only white face in the photos, then after two or three years there was another white face beside his –

the face of his wife, who had married him on his leave in England and followed him to Africa. The District Officer. After that their faces were in so many of the pictures. Mr. Smythe's wife with his wife. The District Officer at the school's Class Day, standing stiffly in his uniform while Mr. Jabi stood beside him in his wrinkled suit and the children lined up beside them waiting for their diplomas. Mr. Smythe and Mr. Jabi at the school Sports' Days.

Mr. Jabi began putting on his trousers, buttoned his shirt. On top of his old wooden dresser, with its bottles of malaria tablets and his soap dish and matches and stumps of candles, there was a newer picture in a metal gilt frame. Mr. Smythe had sent it from England, after Independence, when he'd been transferred back to England and given a pension so that he and his wife could settle down in the country. They were standing in front of a small cottage largely hidden behind shrubs and ivy. They were awkwardly smiling, and he stood as stiffly in his gardening clothes as he had in his uniform. Across the bottom of the picture he had written,

"To my friend and comrade in many an adventure, Albert Jabi. From his old D.O. in fond memory, Tony Smythe."

Thoughtfully Mr. Jabi sat back on the bed and looked around at the things in the room. How would they look to someone else? How did they look to him after so much time? The bed sagged. He was used to it, but it did sag, and the mosquito netting had discolored. The ceiling was dark with soot from the small fires his wife lit when she kept food warm for him on a charcoal brazier. When he had found the time to whitewash the walls he had been too impatient to go on and do the ceiling as well. At least there were new curtains hanging from the rusted wire fastened over the window frame behind the bed. Another piece of the same new cloth swayed in a murmuring conversation with the wind over the opening to the door. The curtains were blue and white, in a pattern that suggested leaves and birds but in reality was only meandering lines and half circles printed on the cloth. He was pleased with the curtains, they dressed up the room a little. But the linoleum was shabby and torn. In places the pattern was worn away. There was nothing to be done about it. He tucked in his shirt, frowned to himself in the small mirror hanging above his dresser and went out to the latrine that stood at the back of his compound.

When he had come back to the room and washed his face in the old china bowl on the wash stand in the corner his wife came in with breakfast for him. She had been up for an hour and she was still perspiring from the heat of the cooking fire. She sat on a hard wooden chair across the room and watched as he ate, fanning herself quietly. She was dressed in a brightly dyed robe, its folds draping themselves over the rungs of the chair.

The breakfast was his usual bowl of boiled grain, curdled milk, and a little honey. He had eaten it so often that it had become like the light splayed across the floor and the bustle of sounds in the dusty air. He would only have noticed it if it had been different.

"How could Tony stay in a room like this now?" he said to her finally, when he had finished half of the bowl.

She straightened up defensively. "I don't think he will see it that way. His own quarters were not so much finer than we have here. The house was larger, but the standard of furnishings was not so different." She had spoken English with him for most of their life together, but she still had a noticeable accent from her own tribal language when she spoke.

"I know how it was for them here, but he's been away. He's been in England. We can be sure he has forgotten how simply we live."

Albert Jabi stared off into the distance as he spoke, gesturing with his spoon. He had kept some of the mannerisms of the classroom, even though he had retired a few years earlier. He was short and slight, but he had never felt uncomfortable with his wife, who was a few inches taller. It had always seemed to him that his position as the village school teacher had made such distinctions meaningless. It wasn't that he was conscious of any sense of personal importance. He was modest, almost diffident, himself, but the work he did, the teaching, seemed to him to be important. The knowledge he had to give to the children was so precious. After they had been associated with each other for two or three years Mr. Smythe had realized to his wonderment that the school teacher, the shy and proper Mr. Jabi, felt that he was playing as important a role in bringing civilization to Africa as Smythe himself did.

"Do you remember," he began again, "it was Tony who brought the linoleum that is still on the floor. We put it down together when he came back from one of his trips."

"Then it will make him feel at home when he sees it again," his wife persisted.

"No. He will only remember that it was so long ago and see that we haven't had the means to put down something new since he left us. I think it must be fifteen years ago that he brought it."

"Will he be so hard on you? He was never that difficult with you before." His wife seemed unworried. He had often envied that in her.

"But the standard he set was so high. It was so very high." He leaned back against the hard chair. He didn't look like a retired teacher when he sat back. He looked simply like a man who was nearly seventy who had worked very hard most of his life and who was concerned about something. "What will he think about all this?"

She shrugged. "I don't think you should worry about it. It will all come out by itself." She was several years younger than her husband, but she had learned to deal with his doubts and hesitations by pretending she had none herself. She had never become accustomed to her role as the school teacher's wife, and when she didn't have to perform any official duties she spent almost all of her time with their children. Her face was almost unlined, but she had become

11

heavier. She wasn't fat, but the weight had given her a further air of dignity and assurance; so she seemed even more certain of what she was saying. Her children who knew her better, understood that she was still the same shy woman from a small village who had been taken from her father's compound to her husband's house without a chance to see anything of any other kind of life. Her husband sometimes didn't seem to notice that despite her manner she depended on him for every decision, and the children had to hide their laughter when he turned to her and asked her to decide what preparations they should make for a trip they'd planned or what they needed to buy for the house.

"It will all come out by itself," she said again. Her robe was a loose swath of material dyed in circular patterns of a rich red against the umber of the cloth. It was her most elaborate robe and she had wrapped her hair in a turban of the same material and put on her best bracelets. She was as nervous as her husband about Mr. Smythe's return to the village, but she concealed it by fussing with her robe's cascade of folds. It was something she never thought about, but she was still a very beautiful woman. Her husband, who sometimes had seemed to neglect her as he worried over his pupils and his school, had never lost his consciousness of her beauty. He sipped his cup of tea, looking at her admiringly over his lifted fingers. His own hair had begun to turn gray, but under the elaborate turban her hair was as black and as crisply curled as it had been the first time he'd seen her.

They hadn't met the first time he'd noticed her. He had come back to his own village after his first year away at training school and he had become aware of her tall, graceful figure in the center of a noisy group of girls coming in from their work in the vegetable gardens close to his father's compound. He found he was too shy to propose to her. He was too shy even to talk to her; so despite his belief, his conviction that such practises had no place in the new Africa he had asked his father to arrange the marriage. The only thing she had understood from their first nervous

12

meeting was that beneath his shyness and discomfort he was very kind and that somehow, incomprehensibly, he was very much in love with her. She had never let him know that she understood how much he loved her. From his side of it he thought it was so obvious it wasn't necessary to say anything.

He looked around and shook his head. "I had such plans for all the things I would do in the house, but I haven't done what I thought I would."

"You have so much else that is wanted from you," his wife responded. As the oldest teacher in the area, one of the two or three left who had taken over their classes at the height of the colonial period, he was in demand for gatherings and conferences. He sometimes thought ruefully that it would have done him much more good to have had some of this traveling when he was still teaching, when he could have shared it with his pupils. He was too self-effacing even to tell his children about his journeys, and often they first learned of a trip or a new honor by reading his name in the papers or hearing him mentioned over the government radio. None of them had remained in the village, but they still came to see him often.

"It doesn't seem like I would have so much to do, but the time goes. It simply goes. I would like to have done so much more to get ready before Tony comes."

They both sat silently for a moment. The curtain over the door continued its swaying discussion with the morning wind, his wife slowly fanned herself, the persistent, faint noise of the chickens scratching outside the window eddied in over the silence.

"I didn't think he would come back," he said finally. "I know he said that he would come back. He said it many times in those last months, but I still didn't think he would do it. Why do you suppose he is returning now?"

His wife went on fanning, waiting for him to answer his own question.

"I didn't think he would be able to accept that his role had become so different. I know he said it was time for Indepen-

13

dence and that he wished us well with everything that lay in the future, but I didn't think he knew himself if he could accept the changes. How could he face being here and not still be in his old position? Sometimes I thought that being our District Officer was more important to him than it was to us. What could he do here, after all? This little country, this small district, all of it so poor and with so little prospect. But he saw his duties as something so much more important."

"You continued to be his friend through all of it," his wife demurred with a wave of her cardboard fan. The picture on the back of it advertized a new powder to help with stomach disorders, but she seemed calmly unaware of its strident message.

"Were we really friends? I often thought about it. I was only the local teacher, and he was the District Officer after all. But I was also the only person in the beginning who could read and write so I suppose we had some common ground."

"But he is coming to see you. After ten years he has made the trip all the way from England to stay with you. You said that to yourself over and over again all those years, 'How can this man be my friend when I am only the school teacher?' I don't know. But I was truly a friend with Beverly, his wife."

"Beverly was so unhappy when she came and she was telling herself all the time to like us."

"No," his wife insisted, "I was a friend of Beverly. In the beginning she came as his wife and she came to my house because I was your wife, but at the end it was different. It was friendship. I'm sorry she won't be with him. We had many things to talk about those years ago while you went out to your meetings and discussions. Just to have you two as husbands was enough to make us friends."

She got up to take his bowl away, ending the discussion. She always went to the market after he'd eaten. He stayed inside his small work room and looked at notes for the next conference he was to attend. But he was too restless to stay in the house. He hadn't seen the house or the things in it

14

with any objectivity for many years, and he realized he hadn't looked at his life with any kind of objectivity for the same long period. He went down the steps from the shaded porch and stood on the hard ground of the compound yard. The sun was already hot, and the torn palm fronds above his head shook with their discomfort. The light was a shining glare that reflected up from the pale, leached earth of the compound. A goat had wormed its way under the corrugated iron fence that surrounded his yard and was noisily pawing at the garbage heap close to the kitchen door.

Mr. Jabi looked around desultorily for a stone to drive it away, but the goat sensed from his movements that it would be better to leave the garbage behind and it flung itself back under the fence, its brown and white body darkened with a layer of dust that it shook off when it was back on the path outside. Mr. Jabi stood thoughtfully, the pebble he'd picked up forgotten in his hand. It would be so different for Tony Smythe to return to the place where he had been so long – but at the same time Albert Jabi wondered about himself. It would be different for him to see the other man as well – and he found to his discomfort that he was no longer certain about who either of them had become.

15

2.

The sounds that woke Mr. Smythe were the same sounds he had heard every time he had made the trip up the river from the coast to the village. He lay on the hard, narrow bunk in the small cabin on the upper deck of the little river steamer, looking up at the wavering gleam that flowed over the peeling, gray painted ceiling above him, listening to the noises. A clanking, annoyed mutter from the engine, an equally irritated answering murmur from the water as the ship forced its way against the current. A hollow scraping of the thin chains that dragged back and forth across their worn pulleys passing new instructions to the rudder. The ship was the same weekly supply vessel he had used when he was on his post. He had ridden it downstream when he had left the post ten years before. The same sounds had wakened him his last morning on the river. The layered texture of the sounds filled the stuffy space around him so completely that it seemed impossible there might be something else beyond the clamoring confines of the cabin. Only the pale shine from the monotonous stream of the water reflected through the porthole onto the drab ceiling brought the presence of the river into him.

He hadn't expected to see the same ship when he had gone to the dock to board. He had been so sure that so much would have changed in the ten years that he'd been gone. At the same time he couldn't imagine it any other way. He told himself to expect that so much would be different, but when he came to the dock he found he still hoped to see the same ungainly little cargo vessel, with its scarred wooden deck and rusted plates, its upper gangway and the row of cabins behind the captain's bridge. He had looked into the captain's quarters with some hesitation, not sure what he would say if he saw someone he recognized, but the captain was new and the crew was the usual casual collection of young men in grease-stained shorts. The captain himself was a middle-aged man who had gotten too fat for his clothes. His skin had an intense dark tone that stood out against the old white paint of the bulkhead where he sat waiting for the last of his weekly cargo to come aboard.

Just as Mr. Jabi had slowly put his feet down on the floor of his house, as if he were seeing its shape and colors for the first time, Mr. Smythe turned on his side and leaned down to pick up his shoes, carefully shaking them to get out any insects that might have crawled inside. He had done it for so many years without thinking – suddenly the gesture seemed incongruous to him. He shook his head, pulled back the mosquito netting and slowly sat up. He looked curiously around him at the small cabin. It was more ramshackle than he remembered, despite obvious efforts to patch up a broken table top and the half-hearted attempts at painting the walls. A new curtain had been hung over the porthole sometime before, but it had already faded to the dispirited lack of color he remembered so well. He stared across the space to the lighted opening. He didn't want to look at the river yet. It was the river, of all the things he'd come back to, that he wanted most strongly to find unchanged.

In his first months away from Africa he had thought that the most intense memories of his life there would fade. When he had returned to England on leaves of absence he had found, like everyone else who has spent any time in the African countryside, that he woke up every sunny morning expecting to feel the burning heat of an African sun and smell the heavy scent of an African village. He had been sure, however, that this consciousness would finally leave him. He thought that within a few months he would have forgotten most of it. He had already learned that the senses – of touch, of smell, of hearing – remembered only imperfectly and forgot so much. But these smells, these sounds hadn't left him. On mornings when he woke to a bright flash of sun on the bedroom floor of his cottage in England he still felt the heat of the other sun, the sun he had left in Africa. He still waited for his nose to detect the raw current of those other smells. When he went to the window there had always been a momentary prick of disappointment when he looked out and saw only their English garden.

His wife had usually been in the bunk above him on their trips back to the station. He washed his face in the small sink in the corner of the cabin and then took a step back and stood for a moment against the empty bunk. With his hand he smoothed its loosely folded sheets. Mr. Smythe was a tall man, but by leaning down he could put his head on the mattress. He smoothed the sheet again and awkwardly bent to put his head on the place he'd stroked. He stood there for a moment feeling the vibrations from the ship's engine through the floorboards, hearing the sounds that had awakened him so many other mornings, his cheek pressed against the stiff surface of the newly ironed sheet.

He didn't want to talk to anyone when he came out of the cabin. He had said hello to the other passengers over their meal the night before, but he had pulled a deck chair off by himself when they sat out in the open space behind the

18

cabins and talked in the evening's abrupt darkness. Breakfast was the usual English fare – eggs and potatoes and pork with some resemblance to bacon. He thought again as he ate that as a meal it wasn't particularly suited to the country, but he and the people who had come there before him had asked for it out of habit and somehow it had become an African custom. He had always liked the breakfasts at Jabi's better – the boiled meal with honey, the sour milk and tea – but he'd never known how to change. He sat for a moment at the battered table when he'd finished; then he finally went out on the gangway, opened the door to the bit of deck above the stern of the ship, and let himself look at the river.

It hadn't changed. The river was just as he remembered it. He breathed in with a sigh that was as much of pleasure as of relief. He had never been able to describe the color of the water to anyone. It was a mottled tone, on some stretches of the river a mixture of green and gray and brown, on others a more flattish brown shade where smaller streams flowed into the current. Close to the banks the colors took on a thickened tone of green. What he remembered even more than the color was the shine of the surface. It was translucent, with a sheen beneath the surface that gleamed just out of reach. In eddies of the stream where the water flowed in steady ripples the surface seemed as though it were made of smoothed marble. The same image of a shining stone surface always came to him when he saw the gleaming water, and the image of flowing water always came to him when he saw polished stone. The two had become a single response in his mind, though he had never known why.

The banks of the river were also just as he had seen them in his mind when he'd daydreamed in their English cottage. On either side of him was a low, shapeless mud bank that held in the meandering gray-green current. The river, like all of the streams in West Africa, flowed through a flat, dusty plain. The surface of the land undulated in small rises and depressions, the rounded slopes not even lifting enough –

19

close to the coast – to be called hills. The river was so sluggish that its level was lifted by the ocean's tides, even though they were now more than a hundred miles upstream. With the tides came salt water, so the current was brackish. It couldn't be used for irrigation. This meant that there were only scattered settlements along the banks, and they'd been built after the first encounters with the Europeans. The banks were covered with mangrove and bushes, behind them were the silhouettes of palms and thorn trees. There were openings in the vegetation now. He could see foot paths winding down to the water's edge and he realized they were passing a village. He leaned over to smell the water, the mingled sharp tang of leaves and earth, and the muskier, coarser smells of the charcoal fires from the huts that were screened from sight by woven fences of dry grass. He smiled to himself, letting the smells fill him. Straightening, he went along the rail until he found a sagging deck chair and pulled it out of the sun so that he could sit alone and look down into the water's glistening folds.

Mr. Smythe had kept his old uniforms when he'd been released from his post, and he had brought things from his kit when he left England. He was sitting in a pair of knee length, rather baggy white shorts and long white stockings that were folded in a broad band just below the knee. He had on a white shirt with the sleeves rolled to the elbow and the collar turned up in the back. The shorts and the stockings had yellowed in the years they'd been stored away and despite a cleaning they still were wrinkled, but it was obvious they'd once been parts of a uniform. The Africans on the ship recognized it and they stayed away from him, but the white passengers felt themselves isolated on the ship and they drew together unconsciously. He was older than any of them. He thought one of them must be some kind of sales agent, two of them were tourists, one was traveling with a

20

camera to collect some material for a travel leaflet. Mr. Smythe had never been heavy, but he'd become even thinner over the years. His face was strongly defined with a clear line of nose and chin and the skin was tightly drawn over his cheekbones. At the temples and over his forehead the hair was thinning and almost white. He was pale, but there was a flushed ruddiness to his skin. He had never tanned in all the years he'd been in the bush. His arms and knees simply got red when he was away from his office. The rest of him had always been covered in one way or other against the sun.

The river's direction shifted and he was moving his deck chair to get away from the sun when one of the men, the photographer, left the small knot of people at a table against the funnel and pulled a chair up beside him. Mr. Smythe didn't want to talk with him, but out of habit he nodded and looked back toward the leaf-covered banks.

"You've been on the river before." The man said it half as a question, half as a statement. His accent was American, but his voice didn't have the hard edge to it that Smythe had gotten used to in London. The other man had probably been living some place outside the United States. Smythe had found that his own accent changed when he spoke only broken English to the people around him.

"That's right," he finally responded, but without any suggestion that he had anything else to add to the statement. The man nodded without answering. After a moment Smythe decided that the other man understood that he didn't want to say anything and wasn't about to break into his silence. Suddenly wanting to talk a little – since he wasn't being pressed to say anything at all – Smythe cleared his throat and gestured toward the tangle of mangrove hiding the bank that was gliding past them.

"I was twenty years on a post upriver. Used to come down on this same supply ship. Hasn't changed at all."

"You must have had a job up there. Missionary?" The man was American, Smythe realized, and once past the first

21

silence he had the American habit of asking questions. Did they really want to know anything, Smythe had wondered when he first heard them loudly questioning each other in London hotel lobbies, or was it some kind of ritual they went through when they met people, like the prayers he had memorized for leavetakings in the villages when he had been going around his district?

Despite his effort to keep his voice casual there was still a lingering consciousness of pride when he finally answered.

"I was the District Officer for the area covering the entire upriver region."

"The old colonial days." The man seemed to understand. "Before Independence?"

Smythe nodded, hoping that the other man would go away.

"Were all you people English?"

"Yes." Mr. Smythe answered with what he thought was an obvious sigh of distaste. "Most of us joined up at university."

"I only ask because I just came through the French colonies." The man seemed momentarily uncomfortable. "They were different," he finished lamely.

"In what way?" Smythe's curiosity overcame his desire to be left alone.

The other man took a moment to answer; then he said with some care, "I got the impression that the French had been busier."

Smythe had been so involved in his own post and his own duties that he had never thought of the French colonial officers who were probably living in villages much like his own a day's journey away.

"Busier in what way?"

"I thought there were more schools, the roads seemed better. You certainly get more of the French language out in the bush."

"We each went about it in our own way," Smythe answered stiffly. "But you must understand," he added after a moment, "we had only the slimmest resources and there

22

was nothing when we came. You must understand that as well. Nothing."

"And you built it up?"

Was there a note of sarcasm in the other man's voice? Smythe looked at him sharply. His face was expressionless.

"Yes," Smythe said with an edge of authority in his voice. "There was nothing here but huts and filth and disease and babies. At least we managed to get some of them into houses."

"You aren't still working?"

Did the other man need to know any of this, or was he only passing the time? Smythe had little small talk, but he had always tried to carry off his end of it when he was with his superiors on their occasional tours of inspection.

"No. I haven't been here since the place went on its own ten years ago."

"But you still have some feelings about it?"

"Yes," Smythe said in a low voice, "yes." They were silent again, staring off into the thick growth on the bank. He was waiting for the other man to say something. He hadn't spoken with anyone for two or three days and he found he did want to talk a little. Even if it was only to this American who seemed to know so little about where he was going. "Do you know," Smythe went on, turning a little in the rickety chair, "the officers were rotated around and we never stayed anywhere long. Except a few of us. Don't know if we were lucky or unlucky. We went back to the same post year in and year out. That was my job. Twenty years in the same district."

"And this is your first time back?"

Smythe nodded, looking again at the leaves, at their dusty green tangle.

"I'd say you have quite an experience ahead of you."

Smythe stood up abruptly and began folding the chair. "Time to get back to the cabin and do some letters." He straightened, brushing his white hair back from his forehead. "It will be that. Quite an experience."

"I'd like to talk to you more about it." The other man was also standing. "When you've finished your letters," he added, stating it as a fact.

"We'll see if there's time before I get to the landing. So much to get ready, things to do," Smythe said vaguely as he made his way back toward the passageway. "So much," he murmured to himself as he opened the door of his cabin. The undulating glitter of the water's reflection still made its way across the ceiling of the cabin, the splotched curtains at the window swayed back and forth as if they were nodding to someone just outside. Feeling himself suddenly perspiring and uneasy on his feet he stretched out on his bunk again. "So much to do," he murmured again. "But nothing at all to do is more like it," and he gave himself over to the sounds that fluttered in the space around him like butterflies with invisible, translucent wings.

3.

It was early, the ship wasn't expected until late morning, but Mr. Jabi left his compound and began walking through the village toward the landing place. His own compound was small, only two buildings, but he kept it fenced in, as the other compounds were fenced in, to have a little privacy in his yard. The path beyond his gate was lined with corrugated iron fences, most of them rusting and dilapidated. Through the gaps he could see into the other compounds, with their bare, swept yards, the open doors of the small buildings, the heaped garbage. He went slowly along the path, stepping around the rubbish that had been thrown outside the fences. It was hot, the sun's glare already blinding. Inside the yards the straggling trees cast mottled patches of shade, and in the center of the village there was a ragged park around the commissioner's office, but on the meandering pathways it was hot.

Mr. Jabi looked around him as he walked. As had happened with his room, he was seeing the village in a way he hadn't for years. It was as though he'd turned over a picture that had been lying face down on a table and there staring up at him was an image that he hadn't expected. He saw that the concrete lining of the drainage canal had broken and begun to crumble. In places the drain was choked with rubbish and tree branches. The branches weren't new. They were leafless, dessicated and withered. They'd fallen into the drain a long time ago and no one had cleaned them out. Tony had been behind the project to build the drain. He'd dug along with the men in the village for the first day or two. Would the others who had worked with him still remember building the drain? Mr. Jabi tried to think of how many of them were still in the village, but it was like trying to separate the tumultuous comings and goings at the entrance to a bee hive. So many people had left; so many new people had come.

The village's one main street, lined with its single-roomed, open-fronted shops, was less dirty, but only because some of the shopkeepers made an effort to keep the space in front of their little businesses clean. He went slowly past the open doorways, nodding to the men leaning against the shadowed counters inside. Everyone knew who he was, even if they had come to the village after he had retired as the school master. They were conscious of his trips to the coast, they were aware of his presence when he was back, even though they never gave any sign that he was noticed. He still seemed like the teacher to them. As he passed he sometimes looked too attentively at them, as if he were going to correct them for doing something they shouldn't. He looked much as he had during his years in the school, and he was sometimes conscious himself when he used one of his old classroom gestures. Then he would laugh deprecatingly and wait for someone else to continue the conversation. Sometimes when he was at conferences of old teachers like himself he would notice that at different points in their discussions each of them would begin to fall back on their old habits and he would catch glimpses of what they must have been like in their village schools in front of their silent, watching students.

26

Mr. Jabi stopped for a moment as he came close to the end of the row of shops. The dirt street was dusty and rutted and so many dried mango pits had been scuffed into the rough surface that it seemed as if it had at one time been pebbled. The two of them had thought so much would change after Independence. He and Tony had laughed when they'd talked about how the village would look. But he could see that it didn't look much different. It had only become shabbier, dirtier, in disrepair. The first thing that was to be done was to pave the street. They had been sure there would be ceremonies, presentations. A speech and the street newly paved. Now after ten years it still was dirt. The dust, as before, was littered with mango pits and with the droppings of the goats and the cattle everywhere.

He walked a few steps further, waited a little, then turned to go back to the center of the village. He usually came this far on his morning walks. The school was only a little distance farther. He let himself come close enough so he could hear the voices of the children reciting, but he never went to the school itself unless the new teacher invited him in for something. He made some of the older children uneasy as they remembered him from their first years in the classroom. The new teacher, one of the newest of the several who had come up from the coast to replace him, lived with Mr. Jabi in a room just off the main house in the small compound. His name was Stanley Morrison, and he had come up from the same training school as Mr. Jabi. Morrison was in his twenties and fit easily into the household. The one luxury Mr. Jabi allowed himself was to sleep late. So the younger teacher would go off by himself to waken the slumbering school.

Tony, his old friend Tony, would be upset at the changes – at the lack of changes. He was sure of it. He could see these things himself, but he didn't want to have to see them. The school had been painted a few years ago – that would look

27

new – that was something. Consciously not looking at the gaping screens and peeled paint on the doorway of the Commissioner's office behind its overgrown garden at the end of the street he turned onto the dirt path that led through the trees to the landing on the river. Before he had gone far he heard someone call to him.

"Jabi." It was a voice he knew. It was the most recent of the District Commissioners who had come to replace Tony. He was standing on the porch of the office gesturing for Mr. Jabi to come to him. Mr. Camara was a large man, already a little fat in the middle, but broad-shouldered and with an impression of strength in his arms and chest. He was round-faced and petulant, peremptory with most of the people in the village, but generally polite to Mr. Jabi, as though he might ask him someday for a reference. His face often had the expression of someone who was seeing himself in an interior mirror as he talked, as if he was unable to forget the vivid impression of his own features.

Mr. Jabi went toward him, worried at the tone in his voice.

"Jabi," the Commissioner repeated, "I see that you are going to the dock."

Mr. Jabi nodded, waiting. Mr. Camara was dressed in tan pressed trousers and a military style shirt of the same material, all of it with the look of a uniform. Mr. Jabi found himself thinking that the Commissioner would probably have looked natural with a swagger stick, like the British officers used to carry.

"I understand that you are to meet someone there." It was a statement of fact. Mr. Jabi nodded, feeling less uncomfortable. It was only this that Mr. Camara wanted to talk to him about.

"I was sent a message that the former D.O. here from the colonial days is to arrive on the ship."

"Yes."

"Perhaps if you had told me, Jabi, we could have prepared some sort of greeting for him. I only had a message last night with some papers brought up in the

28

District car. Mr. Smythe – I think that is the name – paid a visit to the new headquarters of the District Services. He met some of the people there."

"That is possible," Mr. Jabi agreed. He was still standing at the foot of the steps looking up at the Commissioner, but he felt more comfortable a few steps away from him than he would have closer.

"Perhaps you could tell me what he is proposing to do here, Jabi. There's so little for someone to amuse himself with here. I don't know if he will find much to interest him. And as to meeting him it isn't as though we have time to drop what we are doing to do this man's beck and bidding. I think we must be aware of that, as I assume you are aware of it, Jabi."

"Yes," Mr. Jabi answered, "but it has been many years since he was here last, and he will want to see what the improvement has been since you have taken over the position of District Commissioner here. I think we must give him that opportunity."

The Commissioner hesitated. He wasn't used to flattery from Mr. Jabi. It seemed out of place in the other's manner. He shrugged. "I understand your thinking and to a point I do accept it. But I trust that I will have an opportunity to meet Smythe when he has had time to rest himself from his journey."

"Of course," Mr. Jabi said pleasantly.

"Did you know he was ill?" Camara added as he turned to go back into his office. "He spent a day in hospital when he was in the city. Something isn't well with him." And he went through the door.

Mr. Jabi waited a moment to see if the Commissioner had anything more to say; then he turned and went toward the landing again. He was disturbed, but he tried to keep his expression calm and untroubled as he passed other people coming along the path from the river. The Commissioner's

29

wife had begun paying afternoon visits to the new school teacher in his room in the back of Mr. Jabi's compound. It was a small village and there was no way to keep anything hidden for very long. When the visits had begun he had waited for the young man to say something to him, but he never had. Mr. Jabi was now too embarrassed to tell him that the visits should stop since he wasn't supposed to know that they were going on. So he waited every day for the storm that was certain to come. Now he told himself that since Morrison hadn't told him anything he would simply say to the Commissioner that he knew nothing about it.

The Commissioner's wife was more sophisticated than other women who had followed their husbands to the post, but she gave the appearance of having been wounded, somehow, by her loneliness in the village. When Mr. Jabi spent a moment with her he always had the impression that if she were to try to walk quickly she would have a limp, or if she were a bird trying to fly one wing would drag at her side, twisted and useless. So many of the women who had been brought to the village by their husbands had the same wounds. They had fluttered in the anger and confusion that their loneliness had brought on them until their desperation had become obvious even to their husbands. Perhaps the village would have been better administered if the Commissioners had all come alone. It had usually been the plight of the wife that had driven the husband back to the coast and the life there. This time it would be the wife's carelessness, but it was only another side of the same thing. This new Commissioner, however, was more ambitious than the others. He wrote for the newspapers and he traveled for the government – perhaps he would leave before he found out. Mr. Jabi was prepared for the storms, but he would have preferred that they pass over the District in some other direction and leave him and his life in his quiet compound undisturbed.

As he walked on Mr. Jabi found himself still more thoughtful. He hadn't known that Tony was ill. There had been

something in the letter – "as soon as I'm fit and able" – but he hadn't thought about it. If Tony were ill it was too long a trip for him to take. The heat would be too hard on him since he'd been away for so many years. But perhaps this was why he had finally come, after so many years of the usual cards at Christmas and birthdays, with their predictable messages and bright pictures of strange English leaves and berries. Perhaps he was coming because he wasn't well. He needed a change. The medical aid station that they had managed to keep open, sometimes by working in it themselves when they could get no one else, had closed a few months after he had gone back to England. Without his presence no one quite trusted Mr. Jabi's abilities and the village had no funds for even a visiting nurse. If Tony were to get sick they would simply put him on the weekly ship and on its next trip it could take him back to the coast and a hospital. There was nothing else they could do, but since he'd found some way, however unsatisfactory, to deal with the problem, Mr. Jabi straightened and walked a little more quickly. He stayed close to the hanging branches at the edge of the path, not only for the shade, but for the rich smells that clung to them, the odors of dust and sunlight and growing leaves.

The village was on the edge of a large flat island that divided the current of the river into two spreading streams. The island was flat and featureless. It didn't even have the wavering contours of the land on the opposite banks of the river. It was so flat that parts of it were under water during the rainy season, and all of it was suffused with the sense of useless effort this implied. If something were to be built up on many places on the island it would seep away in the next rainy months. Most of the island was covered with a scrub growth of brush and struggling trees, and the village's cattle had long ago stripped away all but the driest and thorniest vegetation. The goats living in the compounds had done the same to most of the bushes and flowers Tony had planted in his efforts to make the village more presentable. The path that Mr. Jabi was following to the river led through a grove of trees and thorny vegetation that forced it to twist from side to side in the shadows.

At the edge of the river there was a long shed that had been built at the same time as the village, and it was still used to store skins and sacks of peanuts and the goods that came in from the ship to the village stores. The area around it was bare and empty, and it was glaringly hot on the open, dust-brown space. A bench had been put up against the side of the shed, set back against the plaster wall so that there was some shade from the overhanging roof. Not far from the shed was the pier, a platform of oil-blackened boards built over pilings of tree trunks driven down into the mud of the river bottom. A few people were already sitting on the bench waiting for the ship, but they moved aside to give him a seat. Their bundles were out on the pier. Mr. Jabi sat back and pulled the top of his shirt away from his chest so that some air could come in, even though the air was as hot in the shade as it was in the sun a few feet away.

He listened to the sound of the people talking around him and to the flutterings of the birds and the distant thump of wooden pestles grinding into mortars as the women worked to get their grain ready for the midday meal. As he had with the sparse furnishings of his room and with the rubbish in the village streets he found himself noticing the sounds, listening to them, wondering how they would sound to someone who had been away for so long. But he couldn't hear anything different. This would be as Tony remembered it, the swirl of water around the trembling pilings, the dip of birds down over the surface of the water pursuing insects, the small group of people sitting against the shed talking until the ship came into sight. Nodding to himself Mr. Jabi settled back, his eyes squinting against the glare, and waited for the sounds of the ship's whistle.

4.

The whistle thundered in the small space of the cabin. Mr. Smythe struggled to force himself awake, his heart racing uncomfortably at the noise. He had fallen into a light doze when he'd come back to the cabin, but the whistle had jerked him awake. Now he could hear the sounds of chains being pulled across the deck, of strainings in the engine room, of voices calling. He tried to get up, but he couldn't quite pull himself into consciousness. He lay back against the sheet breathing irregularly, his hand pressed against his side as he stared up at the ceiling. The current still gleamed above him with its wavering reflection, but it was slower, its movements hesitated. It was coming to a stop, and at the same time the sound of tumult on the deck below him streamed more noisily through the cabin's thin walls.

There was a knock on the door. "Do you know we're coming in to your landing?" It was the American who had been talking to him earlier. He didn't want to see him. He was so agitated with his own emotions that he wanted to be alone before the ship landed. He realized that he would have to answer, since the man had seen him come into the

33

cabin. "Just getting my things together," he called out, hoping his voice sounded properly official. "Be out when the gangplank's down." "See you then," the man answered and his footsteps went away along the gangway and down the stairs. Mr. Smythe pulled himself out of the bunk and sat on its edge, breathing heavily. It was so hot in the confined space. The air seemed to be suffocating him. It would be better outside, but then he would have the sun to contend with. The doctor who had tended him in England had said that the sun would be too much. It had already done enough to him, the man had said. He should let it alone and stay in England where the sun was certainly no danger to anyone. Mr. Smythe began to feel better. He went to the small porthole and pulled back the curtain. The bank drifting past was so familiar to him. As he saw it he felt a sudden pain of remembrance. He had seen it so many times before in his life.

At the place the ship was passing on the bank the thick growth of bushes gave way to a stream that added its flow to the river during the rainy season. A few boats were pulled up on the sand-bar that marked the stream's entrance. They were the same battered home-made boats he had seen there on his other trips so many years ago. He had one of the disturbing moments when it's impossible to tell which manifestation it is you're remembering of the scene before you. How many layers of the memory has the mind peeled away? If he leaned out a little and waited for the ship to move back into the center of the channel he would be able to see the landing. He closed his eyes a moment, deeply moved; then bent forward.

The landing was there, just as he remembered it. The same bound columns of tree trunks that had been driven down into the river bottom and the uneven black wooden platform that had been built over them. There was a line of rubber tires tied against the wooden railing of the pier – some of the tires looked new – there were some new patches of board nailed on the platform. But it was still the

34

old landing. The ship twisted in the channel, sidling toward the pier in a lumbering, sideways motion that the current resisted, as if it were irritated by the ship's clumsy shiftings. As the ship came around he caught a glimpse of the shed where Mr. Jabi was waiting. It had been whitewashed in the last few years, he noticed professionally. Could use a little work on the roof. Then the ship changed direction again and he lost sight of the landing. He pulled his bags up to the door where one of the crew could get them and went out in the blinding heat of the deck, holding his hands cupped over his eyes, looking ahead of him toward the old landing.

Mr. Jabi saw him first, the tall man with thin shoulders in the old-fashioned shorts and knee socks. There were a few other white people on the deck, but he saw that Tony was standing apart from them, waiting behind the crowd of deck passengers who were going to land and who were noisily dragging bundles and cartons toward the ship's railing so they could jump over it as soon as the ship reached the pier. Tony was looking at the crowd waiting in the shadows at the shed, his hands shading his eyes. It was a gesture Mr. Jabi had seen so many times before. He saw that Tony was looking where he was standing and he realized that Tony had also seen him. As usual they didn't wave. They had never waved in all the years Mr. Jabi had come to meet him at the landing. But they were smiling when the ship scraped awkwardly against the line of tires on the edge of the pier and came to a stop.

Tony stood in the turmoil of the deck arranging with one of the boys in the crew to go up and bring his bags. The boy wiped his grease-stained hands on his blackened shirt and went up the steps two at a time, coming out of the cabin a moment later with all three bags under his arms. With Tony behind him he pushed his way through the noisy press of people and deposited the bags on the pier. Tony was paying the boy when Mr. Jabi came through the crowd streaming

35

away over the dusty paths to the village. "Take the things to the compound of Albert Jabi," he said the boy. "We don't want to carry anything in this heat. Ask anyone which is my compound." When the boy looked confused Mr. Jabi repeated the order in his own language, the boy nodded, picked up the bags and hurried off. A little uncomfortably, but with much excitement Mr. Jabi finally turned to Mr. Smythe.

"Tony," he said with a rush of emotion, shaking the other man's hand. "Tony, how are you? Fine. It is good to see you. It is so very good to see you. Fine. How are you?" In his pleasure he was repeating himself, but it didn't matter for the moment. Tony was shaking his hand and he was saying, with as little coherence, "Jabi, old chap, just fine, and you must be fine. It is good to see you, old chap, jolly good, just fine and you are fine too, I can see."

A little self-consciously they stepped back and looked at each other. Mr. Smythe saw the other man's gray hair, the lines on his forehead. "We are getting along a little now. No use denying it. But you haven't changed, Jabi. One would know you anywhere." Mr. Smythe smiled broadly.

Mr. Jabi saw, with some dismay, that the other man was sick. He was pale – Mr. Jabi had expected that – but he looked sallow and tired. He had aged. He was the younger by a few years, but his hair was nearly white and it was thinning at his temples. The impression of vigor that had been so dominant before was gone. His eyes were nervous, shifting their glance from side to side. But the expression in them was warm and pleased. "You haven't changed," Mr. Jabi said finally, "A few gray hairs, but that is only to be expected from men of our age."

"And men of our wisdom, Jabi, of our wisdom." Tony responded in the same mood of easy banter that they had often fallen into when they had met after one of his leaves or one of Mr. Jabi's trips.

"Do you still have the same compound?" he asked as they began walking.

36

"It hasn't changed much since you last saw it. I don't know if you will think we have changed much in any way since you last saw us," he added uncomfortably as they found the dusty path under the trees and began walking slowly through the crowding press of the undergrowth back toward the center of the village.

Smythe's face showed his excitement as they made their way along the path. "Jabi, it is good to be here, d'you know? I should have made the journey years ago. Should have just pulled myself up out of my rut and come down to see the old place. Just the smell of it. Some days I would have given up my garden and the lot just for a smell of the air. Do you know what it is, Jabi? The smell is alive. All I could get there were exhaust fumes in the summers and the gasses from the coal heater in the winters and we had a cottage out beyond the beyond. But this . . ."

Tony stopped suddenly and Mr. Jabi looked at him sharply. Tony laughed loudly and put his hand on the other man's arm. "It really stinks, doesn't it, Jabi? The place really stinks. All that goat shit and garbage and cow piss and the sewer and the Lord himself knows what all. But I missed it – God, Jabi, I missed it." And he laughed again even more loudly and they began walking along the meandering path again. They stayed against the bushes, making way for the small crowd that was struggling away from the ship with their parcels and bundles balanced on heads and shoulders as if they were fleeing a looming disaster that drove them before it with its waves of billowing heat.

Tony walked so slowly that they often stopped in the irregular patches of shade as he looked around him, his eyes shining. At moments he seemed to have forgotten that his friend was with him. Then he would turn on him again. "Jabi, it is good to be here. How are you, old chap? No, you already said that you were fine and I can see it in your face. You're still on top. Jabi – does anyone call you Prince still?"

They both burst into laughter, two old men standing beside a tree laughing noisily in its dusty shade.

"No," Mr. Jabi said when he had got his breath back. "But they haven't forgotten, some of them, and they still look at me this way when they come into my compound." And he gave an imitation of a man coming into a room half blustering and half obsequious, all the time looking wildly out of the corners of his eyes at the person in the room he'd come to see. This started them both laughing so helplessly that people still coming from the boat circled away from the path to keep away from them. Smythe had been presented with the official records of the village school when he'd taken over his post and he had learned that his new school teacher had actually been named – in a rush of enthusiasm for the distant Queen Victoria's dead consort – Prince Albert. Tony had used the term "Prince" a few times when he referred to Mr. Jabi and people in the village had become very upset. Jabi was from another area and nobody knew anything about him, and as far as they were concerned he could be a real prince.

Tony's efforts to smooth the whole thing over had been a complete failure, as he could barely speak the local language and the villagers knew very little English. When he gathered everyone together the elders stood there listening intently and all they could make out of it was that the strange new white man kept pointing to the new school teacher and saying the word "Prince." For a few years it had made it difficult for Mr. Jabi to make friends, but since he never did anything that anyone thought was prince-like it was generally forgotten.

"You mustn't begin that again," he said half-seriously.

"No, no, no, old chap," Tony answered, looking at him and shaking his head. After a moment he said with a nervous self-consciousness, "No, the name will be Albert, when I get used to it."

Mr. Jabi stood looking at him in surprise. The other man had called him by his first name only a few times when they had been involved together in some particularly difficult situation. For the rest of the time he had always been "Jabi," as someone would address an employee or a servant. It had seemed so natural then, so accustomed, that he had never been disturbed by it, but as the years had passed afterwards he had found himself thinking about it with stronger feelings than he expected. Now he understood that Tony was telling him that he had also been thinking about it. The small gestures we shape our lives around, Albert Jabi was thinking to himself, as they went on toward the center of the village.

Albert didn't need to have worried that Tony was going to see the dirt and the disrepair of the village. Tony would see it another time, but now as his head turned from side to side and he peered into doorways and over the fences of the compounds he saw only himself. He saw the young District Officer coming to take over a post, unsure of himself and how he would do, but sure in every way of the necessity of the job itself. He could feel himself turning into the street when he first had come off the boat and walked toward his office, the string of boys struggling behind him with his gear looking like a two-dozen-legged insect that had gotten tangled in some cotton batting. Many people thought the men who went into the Colonial Service were the family failures, and they wound up in the bush in the back end of one of the British colonies through a sheer inertia of mediocrity. Some of the men who drifted into the Service fit the description, but just as many of them who had come into it were like Tony, idealistic, enthusiastic, and rather ambitious. In 1937, when he'd been accepted for the post, just out of Cambridge, it was a good job. The pay was good, a man could work up – since everyone felt that the colonies were there to stay – and if he did get fed up there was always the chance to get something better paid with one of the commercial firms.

Like most of the new appointees Tony's school grades

had been average and he'd spent more time than he should with sports, but when he'd gone back to Cambridge for the additional year of training after he'd been accepted for the job he'd taken it seriously. For some of the new men the Colonial Service Course wasn't that important, but he'd taken it on as an additional chapter of Holy Writ, from the classes in soil conservation to the rudiments they'd given him of law and courtroom procedures. Then, just as he was ready to bring everything he'd learned to the tribes of Africa, 1939 came, and he didn't finally get his appointment until 1945, after he'd done his years in the Navy. The village had been his third post, but the first two had been only temporary arrangements while he took over for someone else for a few months.

It was never the policy to leave someone on a post for too long a time; so he'd been shifted to other areas once or twice in the early years, but then he'd always found himself back in his old office again and after a time he didn't think much about being moved. He believed, secretly, that he'd been forgotten, but since he was where he wanted to be and they hadn't forgotten him to the extent of neglecting his pay and his leaves he'd become part of the life of the village; though he would sometimes have found it difficult to say clearly what his role was.

When he was on the Coast, however, waiting to go on leave or conducting some business in the offices of the Colony he didn't find he was much different from the others that he met. Even if they hadn't had so many years on one post they still had come to know people where they were, they had made a life there. He sometimes thought of his own experience as simply representative of what they had all been through when they had taken over their posts, only his had gone on longer. He had been almost unaware of Independence – or even the possibility of it. Much of his responsibility was theoretically to prepare the people of his area to take over the running of their own lives, but he was so busy with his own work that he never found time for this part of the job. Independence had interrupted him in the middle of a sentence. He still felt a sense of exasperation about it, even if he couldn't remember any more what the sentence was about.

The children who were too young to be in school hung in the doorways as they passed. Albert tried to wave them away, not wanting them to disturb Tony as he looked around him, but he realized with a start that the younger children – if they hadn't left the village – had never seen a white person. After Tony had left there had been occasional white visitors for two or three years, but then they'd stopped coming. A group of children in ragged clothes hurried out of one of the compound gates and came toward them with some uncertainty. They held out their hands to him then trying to use the school English they heard from their older brothers and sisters they looked bravely up at him and said, "Goodbye." In their nervousness they'd gotten their greetings confused. Tony stopped, took their hands seriously, his body looking even more ungainly in the baggy shorts as he bent over them. "Hello," he said slowly and distinctly three or four times. After a moment embarrassment overcame the group and they scurried back into the compound shrieking with excitement.

"Ah Jabi – Albert – " Tony said as he watched them. "It could be that first day when I came to you here. It gives me a feeling – " He fell silent. "But it isn't that day now. It's another day, and we've both come a long way. What do you think will come next, Albert? You must have thought about it. What do you think will come next?" He started walking again. "God, it's hot. Albert, how did I stand it all those years?"

5.

Mr. Jabi's wife was waiting at the compound gate and she hurried out towards them, pulling the hem of her long robe up over her arm so she could walk faster. She held out her hand, so pleased to see Mr. Smythe that for a moment she could remember only her most stilted school English. "It is so good that you could come to visit us here," she finally managed, smiling so broadly that Mr. Smythe found himself thinking that she looked even younger than she had when he'd known her before. In a moment she would see his pallor, his white hair, the slowness of his step, as he would see her heavier body and her lined face, but in their first pleasure at seeing each other again they paid no attention to the marks that the years had left on them.

"Shouldn't have waited so long to make the trip," he said, still shaking her hand. "Don't know why we never arranged for you and Albert to come and visit us there."

She hesitated as he used her husband's first name, then smiled again as she saw her husband nodding. "It would have been too long a way to go for myself and Albert. I'm glad you have come instead."

"Not a moment too soon," Smythe agreed, "But you've got to get me in out of the sun or I will faint dead away outside your gate. I'm not used to the heat anymore."

They crossed the small trampled space to the house, walked up the steps to the porch and went into the sitting room, which hadn't been changed since Tony had left. He stood looking around him, still smiling; then dropped into the hard-backed chair beside the table where he'd usually sat. "Can't believe I'm back, you know. I expected so many changes."

"We must have something to eat," Mr. Jabi's wife went toward the kitchen. "I know about the food on the boat so I know you didn't eat."

"No, I didn't," Tony laughed, "Just a little breakfast. Everybody knows about the food on the boat. But let it go a moment. Little something for you."

He opened one of the bags that the boy had left in the room and began rummaging through it. He pulled out a wrapped package and handed it to Albert. "Something that came from the cottage. Souvenir you might call it."

Albert stood at the table unwrapping the package, his wife beside him. Inside it was an elaborately worked silver dish. It was so much more than anything they might have expected that they were silent.

"I don't know what to say, except thank you," Mr. Jabi said finally.

"It is so fine. You know we have nothing that is so fine in the house," his wife said in a rush.

Tony held up his hands, trying to look casual. "Not worth fussing over. Just something I noticed as I was packing my bags." For a moment he was thoughtful. "Didn't know who else I might have given it to if the truth were known."

Mr. Smythe's wife, Beverly, had called Mr. Jabi's wife Nindi. He had never used the name himself, but he was impatient with the old habits of ceremony that still clung to him even

43

though the job had been finished for so many years. He wanted the habits to be over, even though he understood that they would continue to creep back if he didn't keep a watch over them. He would have to remind himself to call her Nindi. Simple as that. He'd have it in a few days. Just like everything else he'd had to learn when he'd taken over his post. If he weren't too old to learn now, he said to himself, leaning against the chair's stiff back and looking around at the familiar room. They had left him alone while they busied themselves over lunch. He knew that Albert wouldn't be expected to help with the cooking or the serving, but his old friend had said he'd find them something to drink and he'd followed his wife through the hanging curtain into the back of the house. The room where Tony was sitting was shaded and cool, much cooler than the air outside, but the glare from the bare earth of the yard was reflected through the windows into the space around him, lightening it and filling it at the same time. The light dominated the space around him, even though he was shielded from it by the walls of the house. He'd have to get used to it again – to the sun and light. A few days. A few days would see to everything.

He could see into the smaller room leading off from the room where he was sitting. It had been Mr. Jabi's office – library he'd jokingly called it – when he was a teacher. His desk was still against the wall and its worn surface was as crowded with papers, opened books, pencils, and calendars as it had been then. He had the impression that his friend's life was still as busy, unless – Mr. Smythe smiled to himself – the papers had simply sat there untouched since Mr. Jabi had been given his pension. The same map of the old district hung over the desk. He could see the spindly web of lines that marked the roads. That also looked the same, but it must have changed by now. They couldn't still be using the old road map.

Mr. Jabi came into the room with a pitcher and glasses. "I've orange squash for us. You always used to drink it. The

44

water has been boiled and then left to go cool and I don't think it will do you any harm."

The lunch Mr. Jabi's wife brought was served in two porcelain bowls with saucers over them to keep them warm. She also had a thin loaf of bread, cut into two pieces. When Tony lifted the saucer the room filled with the smell of spices. As he'd expected it was cooked meat, pungent with bits of peppers, the whole dish poured over rice that filled the bottom of the bowl. Nindi didn't eat – she had never eaten at the same table with them – but she sat across the room watching, her face still smiling broadly.

Tony looked toward her and nodded. "Smells as good as I remember." Then he added, almost as an afterthought. "Must remember to call you by your proper name, as Beverly did." He looked down at his food and carefully lifted his spoon, aware that Mr. Jabi was staring at him, but they were hungry, it was past lunch time, and they ate without saying anything more. He had forgotten how good the food could taste. He knew they would have the same thing to eat every day and he would get tired of it, as he always did, but for the moment he didn't care. He ate with pleased vigor, then pushed his bowl aside, leaned back in his chair and looked across the table.

"You'll have to tell me something about the state of the village now."

"I'm not in so close contact as I was before," Mr. Jabi demurred.

"But I'm sure you can fill me in. I don't need the particulars. Just a general impression will do. Though if you do have a figure or two it will help me to get a clearer grip. I don't expect to be able to put it together all at once."

As Mr. Jabi tried to think of something to say his wife said suddenly, "Please . . . Tony," interrupting them for the first time in her life. She was clearly uncomfortable using his first name but she persisted. "Tony, if you can excuse me. Can you tell us about Beverly?" It was silent in the room. Tony looked down at his hands; then he shifted in his chair. He was conscious of the sounds drifting in through the open window, the desultory noises of the village when a meal had just finished. A donkey brayed and the sound seemed to him – as it had sometimes before – to resemble a grotesque sob.

"We would like to know," Mrs. Jabi said apologetically.

"She should have come with me, as you know," he finally began. "She was very keen on the idea. She talked a lot about it and we'd begun to lay some plans. Don't know how so much time went by without either of us noticing it. It does if you're not careful." He was silent again. The others watched his face as he stared off into the light beyond the window, the thumb of one hand carefully rubbing the knuckles of the other.

"I thought she would come," Albert said after a moment, uncomfortable with the hesitations.

"Yes, she was set on it," Tony finally continued. He breathed deeply, lifted his shoulders, looked down at his hands again. "I haven't talked with anyone, you understand, just the people on her side of the family so it's hard to know where to start. It wasn't anything she brought with her from here. That's something, at least. She was always so concerned about seeing to her health when she was here. I was the sickly one for a time after we'd returned to England. Had fever and a bad throat that lasted me through most of the first year. Never could go anywhere without wrapping myself up in a sweater. But she never felt it. She'd been so strong here and she was the strong one there. Never ran down. But it was cancer. We didn't know it at first. It was only that she didn't seem to have the same energy, and she'd always been one for keeping busy. But there it is. You never know."

He fell silent again, moving a little in the chair. He looked down at the floor and almost diffidently rubbed the back of one hand against the side of his face.

"Was it hard for her?" Mr. Jabi asked finally.

Tony was still silent; then he forced himself to continue. "How close we all were in the years I was here. You two and Beverly and me. I don't think at the time I had any idea.

46

Often you don't. Things just take their course. I haven't told any of this to anyone, but I must tell you about the last days, even if I don't tell anyone else. She knew I would come here finally. She told me to see you and tell you she had thought of you and she wanted to make the journey with me."

They sat unmoving in the strange reflected light of the room, as motionless as if a scroll were being unrolled, a turn at a time, and it was they themselves who were the figures painted on the scroll. He was still holding his head up, but he had begun to cry quietly and there was a dull glistening of tears on his cheeks. Embarrassed, Mr. Jabi rose and went toward a cabinet in the corner of the room to search for a handkerchief.

"No," Mr. Smythe protested. "I have something." He bent down and rummaged in his bag. "Bad show to lose my grip after all this journeying. It hasn't been so long, you know. Just two months now. You think something can never happen to you. It can't pass your way and then it does and you think you won't be able to stand it and then it has passed and you can sit with friends and say 'Just two months ago now' and it sounds natural. And it is natural," he repeated with an insistent tone, "no matter how hard it seems at the time. You know, Jabi, just like all those poor chaps who lost someone in the little clinic we tried to set up. They cried, some of them, and we'd heard so much nonsense about how they were as tough as a stick."

He leaned back and wiped his eyes again with the hand-kerchief, shrugging apologetically.

"Had to come all this way to find someone I could talk to about it," he said with a rueful lift of his arms. "I know she wanted me to say something to you. It was so very hard for her. It was so damned hard for her. I thought I would go crazy sitting in the room beside the bed watching her. I think at the end she was almost crazy herself. She didn't know me when they finally began giving her enough of the drugs so that the pain wouldn't kill her."

"I am so very sorry," Nindi murmured after another

47

pause. "I should have tried to come and nurse her, but there was only one letter from you then and you wrote it was alright. You said it wasn't anything we need worry over."

"I didn't think it was so bad. The damned sickness just begins and then it goes all crazy and it's over before you know it. But at the end, when she was still able to talk, she did ask about you. She did ask about the post here. Wanted to know everything. It didn't matter when it had happened. Anything I could tell her. I sat in the room and talked until I was hoarse. All the things that we'd done together, the four of us. It didn't matter when it had been. I could see that it was all the same to her. A year before, ten years before. I could begin anywhere. I just had to keep talking until the pain was too much and then I'd ring for the nurse."

His voice dropped and he seemed almost to forget they were in the room.

"The last day she kept telling me to go and get the children so she could touch them and talk to them just for a last time. You know? She wanted the children."

He had turned so he was looking down at the table. He pressed his closed hand down on the surface and the fingers slowly unclenched, as if the strength were going out of them. "But you know how far we got with that." His voice was resigned. "No use bringing it all up again, I suppose, but I did have to tell her there weren't any children. That there never had been any children. And she didn't want to believe what I was telling her. So we started to argue, there in the room, and she was so pale and so thin I couldn't really bring myself to look at her. Then I think she decided I wasn't pretending and there weren't any children to see. She became very quiet. She didn't say anything. I started to talk again about the life here but she lifted her hand and I could see she really didn't want to know any more. The next day it was so hard for her the doctor had to give her more drugs so that was really the last time we had a chance to say anything to each other. A bit disappointing for it all to come down to that when time was running out, you know?"

48

Mr. Jabi nodded. He was trying not to cry himself. His wife was wiping her eyes with her face half turned, not wanting Mr. Smythe to see her.

"How are your children, Jab – Albert," he asked after a pause. He looked from one to the other. "Albert. Nindi. I'll have it down in a day or two."

Albert cleared his throat. "All are well, thank you. Only one lives not far from us. You knew our youngest daughter. She is further up the river in the Commissioner's office there. The others are all in the city. Perhaps you had a chance to see them when you were on the coast?"

"No. I couldn't be sure that any of them would remember an old man like me. I wasn't that old when I saw them last but they would regard it in a different light. But you aren't the parents of parents, as we used to say?" He was trying to be briskly in control again.

"Yes," Nindi answered, still dabbing her eyes with a hand-kerchief she'd taken from the sleeve of her robe. "There are two new small ones at the home of our oldest daughter."

"Another sure way to tell we're getting older. I want to have a chance to chuck them under the chin before the trip's over, even if having them around does mean that our own days are getting shorter. She asked me about them. Something else she wanted me to talk to her about in the last few days she had. Anything I could think of about those children of yours. We didn't have a letter for quite a long time and she wanted to know the news. Now you've told me and I don't have any way of passing it on." He looked up suddenly and his face was wet again. "But it does ease it a bit to talk. Didn't expect though," he said wonderingly, "that this would be the only place I could come to talk about it with anyone. Don't know what that all means, Albert. You used to be able to explain things. Perhaps you can explain this as well."

6.

Mr. Smythe napped for the rest of the afternoon. They had put sheets on a bed for him in one of their children's rooms. It was behind the sitting room at the end of a short corridor, next to the room that Mr. Morrison, the new teacher, rented from them at the back of the house. The room was dark, its only decoration the long lengths of curtain that swung in the casual breeze. As he slept Mr. Jabi and his wife moved carefully through the rest of the house, trying not to disturb him. The afternoon lengthened, the sun yellowed and dried. There was a persistent lowing of cattle that had been left tied in the compounds as they smelled the herds that had been driven into the brush to graze coming back into the village. The sun's light glanced across the fences of woven dried grass and in the darkening shine the grass looked golden and gleaming, as if it were living again.

Albert was sitting at his desk going through his schedule of conferences when he heard someone come onto the porch. He paid no attention. His wife had gone to the market and he assumed she was coming back. He was scheduled to be part of a conference in three weeks and he was trying to think of something different to say. He began to write a note to himself when he heard someone laugh at his shoulder.

"Jabi, you are still a working man."

He looked up and saw a heavy, gray-haired man in light trousers and a brown daishiki leaning over him, reading what he had just written.

"Suso." He held out his hand and the other man shook it. "I am surprised to see you."

"I thought you might send for some of us, but I had to come and see Tony for myself. I can hardly believe that he has come to us again."

"Sit, come and sit, Suso," Albert insisted, getting up and leading him into the other room. Suso settled slowly into a chair by the table. He reached over and picked up the silver bowl that was still sitting beside its opened wrappings, like an archaeological specimen that was waiting for classification.

"That must be English and it must be from Tony." He looked at Albert questioningly. Albert nodded, uncomfortable that the gift should have been left out on the table for someone to see. It was something they had wanted to keep only for themselves – now, he knew, it would in a subtle way become the property of the village. He reached out for it and put it back in the box. Even though it was now common property he still didn't want anyone else to see it. Suso leaned back in his chair and pointed to the bags that were pushed against the wall.

"I see Tony's kit as well; so it must be true. He has come back." Mr. Suso shook his head and looked over at Mr. Jabi. "The word had come up from the coast that he would be here and one of the boys who was on the boat said he had seen him, but still – after so long a time! What do you think, Jabi?"

"He is having a nap now. He isn't used to the sun. I think it was a bit too much for him."

"And Beverly has died and he is not a well man himself." In a small village all news goes immediately from household

51

to household. Like the dust it seeps under the walls and makes its way in through the windows. It thickens the texture of the air, it is part of the breath that stirs the leaves of the bushes.

"Beverly died two months ago. He said they were planning to make the trip together, but then it was discovered that she was very sick and she was unable to leave her bed. Now he has been to a doctor on the coast, I believe, but I know very little about it."

Albert looked down at the floor, his face without expression. He knew that anything Tony told him belonged to other people who would come to the compound, but he still had wanted to keep some of it to himself, just as he had wanted the little bowl to be free of scrutiny. There was a step outside on the stairs again and this time it was his wife, perspiring from the heat, a basket of fruit on her head. She nodded to Mr. Suso.

"You have been shopping, I see," Suso began in a normal voice, but she lifted the basket down and shook her head.

"Tony is having a nap," she whispered.

"So I understand," Mr. Suso said nodding, his voice lower. "I will sit until he wakens."

Mr. Suso – Mado Suso – went to sit on the porch, fanning himself as he looked out into the dusty yard. He had sometimes worked closely with Tony when the other man had been the District Officer, but he had always felt so uncomfortable around him that they hadn't become friends until the last year or so before Tony was to leave. Mr. Suso sighed, unbuttoning the top button of his trousers under the loose daishiki so he could sit more comfortably. He perspired more in the heat now; he knew he was overweight, but he told himself he was past the point in his life where he could be expected to do anything about it. He wiped his face with his handkerchief and sat back in his chair to wait.

It is impossible for anyone who has some kind of authority

52

over someone else not to use the authority at some time, however much they try to disguise it from themselves. The local officers who spent their lives on isolated posts in the African colonies were in theory only working with the tribal leaders in their districts to bring about a "general betterment." The assumption was that there was some agreement, however vague, on what this meant. In reality there were so few white administrators – often one man with a tenuous jurisdiction over an area with forty or fifty thousand Africans – that they had to leave much of the real responsibility for what happened in their districts to the local tribal leaders. The temptation to meddle, however, was usually too strong to overcome, and there was sometimes strong pressure on the tribes to make them elect some kind of chief by what the District Officers called "the democratic process." Most small villages were loosely run by a council of Elders and the idea of giving up their authority to a "chief" was so dismaying that they spent a number of meetings discussing how they would deal with this. Since they expected some kind of benefit from their relationship with the local administrator they didn't want to offend him, but at the same time the idea of electing a chief was unacceptable – at least in the way the District Officer was insisting on, since it meant giving up their own authority. The solution to the dilemma – in other villages like this one – had been the election of someone like Mr. Suso.

At the beginning Tony would have accepted whatever leader the village chose, but for several months there was wrangling among the Elders. Then while he was off on the coast they decided to let the one man of some wealth and authority in the village be named as chief, and at the same time Tony returned filled with ideas of village elections that he'd been lectured about by his superiors. Since he now wanted to have a public election the man they had chosen declined, refusing to go through the motions of being presented to the village and having his affairs discussed by his neighbors. The Elders realized that they had to do something so they decided to "elect" Mado Suso. He became

53

"chief" of the village for most of the period that Tony Smythe had been its District Officer. The Elders had chosen Suso because he had been to a missionary school and could read and write a little, because he had lived on the coast and was "worldly" by the village's standards, and because he had an English suit, which was very hot to wear but looked impressive at ceremonies. Suso had tried to refuse the honor, but he had finally been convinced when the entire gathering of the Elders told him that his children would benefit from his sacrifice for the village's peace. When this was put in more specific terms – his children would be given the crops grown on a common field tilled by the people of the village – he gave way and presented himself at Tony's office with a group of Elders who announced that the village had "elected" a chief.

For some months there had been considerable anxiety in the village as people waited to see if the District Officer would accept the "chief." At first Tony had been difficult to deal with. He often questioned Mr. Suso when he came to inform him of some decision of the Elders. Who had voted for this, who had voted against it. But then he was seen to take Mr. Suso by the hand, the petitions that Mr. Suso brought to him were taken with complete seriousness, and often there was some visible result. Everyone sighed with relief, and the lines of communication between Tony and the people in his district became much more open. At times, even, Mr. Suso assumed some of the authority of a chief when the man who had declined the position had to be away on business.

Tony, for his part, sitting in his hot room with its dirt floor, trying to keep up some semblance of authority as perspiration soaked his shirt and the boys working the fans above his head laughed to themselves over his discomfort, realized that something was happening that he didn't quite understand. Like most other District Officers confronted with the same situation he asked his house boys what was happening, and from their vaguely disingenuous answers he pieced

54

together enough to understand Mr. Suso's role. He was intelligent enough to accept that this was all he was going to be able to see of the village's workings; so he simply went along with it. His only personal response had been sometimes to heap more praise on Mr. Suso than the situation called for, which made him more and more embarrassed, while the real figure of authority in the village became annoyed and often jealous, which Tony noted out of the corner of his eye. For Mr. Suso it was a difficult and demanding period of his life, despite the additional food that had streamed into the household, and he had been as excited as the most doctrinaire nationalist when Independence finally came to the village.

There were noises of firewood being chopped, of animals being milked, of grain being pounded as the shadows stretched further and further over the deepening yellow of the dust and the sun turned into a red globe suspended in a haze at the horizon. Tony was asleep, but the porch where Mr. Suso was sitting and the room inside the house began to be filled with men sitting in the shadows and talking with lowered voices. Albert went from group to group, greeting everyone who had come. He was almost as surprised by the gathering as he was by Tony's arrival itself. As he looked around his crowded rooms he realized that every man who had been living in the village when Tony was its District Officer had come to the house. Only a few of the Elders were still living, but they too had gathered with the others. For a long period, when it had become clear that Independence was inevitable, people had drawn away from Tony and only the school teacher had continued to be his friend. There was then some grumbling in the village against Albert as well, but he had known Tony too many years to desert him. Now everyone was here again in his house, but Albert felt no urge to remind them of things they'd said ten years before. He was only glad to see them all. He had even left the silver bowl out on the table beside its box. As it was passed from hand to hand it became somehow the property of the whole village, but this seemed part of the moment's sense of expectation.

The whispering stopped when they heard a shuffling from the room where Tony had been napping. When he finally emerged through the doorway, still in his creased shorts and knee stockings, brushing his white hair back from his forehead, there was a burst of noise. Everyone stood up at once and went toward him. They crowded together, bumped against the table, knocked over a chair. Tony's expression was a blank surprise. Albert found himself backed into a corner as the others pressed past him; so he had no chance to say anything. Then Tony recognized the faces, he saw who had come to greet him. He began to call their names, he shook hands, he asked after wives and children, he joked with the men he'd known the longest. Laughing he put his arms over shoulders, his smiling white face taller than theirs by a few inches. He looked over at Albert.

"Do you see who we've got here, Albert? The same lot that used to hang about the office keeping me from getting at my work with all their petitions and what not. Now they've turned up again and it isn't even office hours. I'd say turn them all out so we can have a little quiet. Time in the morning to listen to all the complaints." And he beamed and shook everyone's hand again. He was surprised himself that he remembered every name, that he could talk about their families, that he still knew enough to ask them about their shops and their travels. He had been part of the village in ways he hadn't understood himself.

"We meet again, Tony," Mr. Suso said when there was a pause. "We heard from Jabi that you were thinking of returning; then there was word from the coast that you'd been seen there on your way to us, and a few people said they had seen you on the boat – but we couldn't believe it so we had to come to see for ourselves."

Standing against the table with the laughing faces around

him Tony seemed for a moment overcome by the emotions of it all. Then he took a breath and smiled.

"If it's a petition you've come with or one of those arguments about whose cow got into whose compound or a case of someone failing to keep his promise about a bride price I'm sorry but this time you'll have to sort it out yourselves. You can come back in the morning but I won't have any more to tell you then than I do now."

There was more laughter and a few of the men applauded. "Furthermore," he was laughing himself, his eyes shining with pleasure, "I must remind you that this is past office hours. It's past sundown and that is the sacred time when the District Officer must confer with his evening drink."

There was laughter again. As the men grew quiet they looked toward Mr. Suso and he understood that he was expected to make a last welcoming speech to Mr. Smythe for the village.

"It is true that we have come to pay our respects, but this time we have no petitions and no matters of importance to take up. It has been many years since we have seen you. Ten, it is, I believe. Now that you are back I must say for myself that I think more often of all the years you were with us than I do of the years that you have been gone."

"There at the end I had a strong impression that you were glad to see me go." Tony's voice had a touch of peevishness.

"Not you," Suso protested. "Do you know it was at the end that we came to understand that we had two separate things? We had a representative of the colonial government in the office at the end of the street, and we had Tony Smythe who we knew so well in his quarters. We had to keep the two of you separate, even if there was just one person who was both of these things. It was confusing at some moments."

"It wasn't me who got it mixed up."

"No, no, no. I don't think you got anything mixed up any time any of us can remember. But, still, it was hard for us to

57

keep the two different sides of you separate."

"I didn't think of it that way. I was just as I'd always been, sweating away in the office trying to keep the whole thing from falling to pieces. When I'd get to thinking, there, I've got it running – in you'd come with some petition or some new idea about how to do it all and I'd have to take the next week to get it straight again." He threw up his hands in a gesture of mock despair, grinning broadly at all of them. "I got the same speech at every village when I was out on tour – don't know where you chaps got your little talks. I sometimes thought you must have learned them from a book. Something about your hearts being heavy if I couldn't listen to your petition and that you would accompany me on the beginning of my journey but you would grieve until you would see me coming again with the answers you most earnestly prayed I would give."

He had mimicked the tone of a tribal Elder and they laughed uproariously at his imitation. They had fallen into the same tone of easy banter he remembered so well from his years with them. Mr. Suso spoke again.

"If I may be disrespectful, you had an answer which we also heard every time."

Tony suddenly laughed with them and straightened to his full height. As he'd done hundreds of times before he folded his arms across his chest and looked at them solemnly. "I give you every assurance," he began, his tones measured, "that Her Majesty's government has a personal awareness of your grievance and that no stone will be left unturned in its endeavours to see that right and justice are brought to this distant corner of Her Majesty's empire."

There was another burst of laughter and applause. He shook his head.

"There was only one of me, you understand." He looked at the faces around him. "I know it must have got a bit sticky there at the end with all kinds of things being said, but I always knew where I stood."

"Yes," Mr. Suso replied a little uncomfortably, "We knew

that it was you we had to deal with, and that didn't make it any easier; since we'd known you so long and so well, and so much else was changing."

It had become darker in the room and there were deep shadows beyond the window and the doorway. Albert brought a lantern in from his study, lit the wick and put it in the center of the table.

"Don't you have electricity now," Tony asked in surprise, turning from his conversation with Suso.

"Yes, we do," Albert smiled, "but I thought this would make you feel more like the old times."

An hour after sunset, when life in the village was gathered around the few little shopping stalls, there was a noise at the gate and an older man with three younger men, almost boys, clustered around him made his way into the compound and stepped onto the porch. There was a silence and the men inside the room close to Tony made an opening for the man to come toward him. He was wiry and thin, very dark-skinned, wearing a long blue robe sewn with strips of silver ornament around the neck and sleeves and an embroidered hat. Tony hesitated, then held out his hand.

"Alhaji," he said.

It was the term for a Moslem who had made the pilgrimage to Mecca. The man had made the trip while Tony was District Officer and they'd welcomed him back with drums and dancing. It was he who had been the real figure of authority in the village while Suso had acted as his sur-rogate in dealings with Tony.

"Mr. Smythe," The Alhaji answered. "We welcome you back to the place where you were among us so many years."

Assuming his role again Tony nodded gravely. "I am honored that you should come to greet me."

The Alhaji looked around him. The younger men, his sons, nodded to the others and then disappeared on the porch again, leaving the scene to their elders.

"We did not meet so often when you were here before," the Alhaji said.

"I did not have the honor then," Tony answered, then he nodded toward Mr. Suso, who was standing close to him by the table, fanning himself with one of Mr. Jabi's writing tablets. "Mr. Suso, I believe, brought your messages to me at that time."

"You understood then."

"I understood enough."

"Whatever you understood you have given us pleasure by returning," the Alhaji said with a solemnity that was half serious, half mocking.

"Suso just said it was a bit of bother for you at the end to have to deal with the D.O."

Suso looked away, a little embarrassed at being part of their talk. "I said only that we decided it was less of a difficulty for us if we thought of our friend Tony as one thing and the job of District Officer as another."

"And you didn't care for this?" the Alhaji asked, watching his face.

"Certainly not! You can't cut someone up into pieces like that. For better or worse I was what I was."

"Yes. We understand it. But you can understand that we wished to make the last months easier for all of us. We could trust you in a personal way, even if we had lost faith in your job."

"The two were the same," Tony persisted.

"Yes, I think they were," the Alhaji said with a shrug, "but let me say it is much easier for me to come and greet you now than it was then when I had to pretend to be only one of the village Elders."

"And Beverly . . ." Suso began.

"I will bring in glasses and cups. We have to have something to drink," Albert broke in. "There is water in the vase. There will be tea, I think, and there is orange squash if someone wants to have a taste of the old days. Will it be orange squash for you, Tony?"

60

7.

It was the sounds that woke Tony in the morning, the elaborate composition of sounds that had wakened Albert the morning before, that had wakened each of them all the mornings that they had lived in the village. It began with the faint background, thinly sketched, of birds stirring in the trees as the first light reached the dusty branches where they'd perched. Then against the background, in stronger tones, the tentative squawking of chickens close to the houses. After that, in a burst of strong yellows and reds, as violently hued as the sky itself, the raw sound of roosters crowing, first in one compound, then answering from one to another. The air was still soggy with dew, but already the first yellow stream of sunlight was drawing the moisture out of the earth and the leaves. Mingled with the bleating of the goats and the bawling of the monkeys was the first murmuring from the women's quarters, the separate rooms in each of the compounds where the women slept with the children. The framework for the morning was set up clumsily, without any seeming order, but its scaffolding was erected in a few moments, the job done, and the day could begin.

Tony lay for a moment when he had wakened. He turned his head to look at the tendrils of sun reaching into the room. He leaned over and groped for his shoes, shaking them to get the insects out. He pulled the mosquito netting open and stretched his legs over the side of the bed. It seemed so natural for him to hear the sounds that for several moments he only half noticed them. Then he stopped, fully hearing them for the first time. He sat without moving on the sagging mattress, open-mouthed with surprise at the depth of his emotions. He had wakened to these sounds so many mornings that they had become part of his consciousness – just as the lines the sun had left on him still ringed the corners of his eyes. The sounds around his English cottage had never been so vivid. They had been muffled somehow in the thick mat of leaves and grass below his window. It was this intensity of sounds that he had missed, and he felt himself wakening in a way that he hadn't in all the years he'd been away from it.

When he finally pulled himself off the bed he moved slowly around the room. Like Albert the day before he was seeing everything with a fresh clarity. The room was more bare than Albert's. There were no family pictures but he had put a photograph of his wife on the small table beside the bed before falling asleep. Her face was close to him. On the whitewashed walls there were small Christian lithographs. Christ with a swollen red heart, the Virgin in yards of flowing garments. Albert was one of the few Christians in the village, but he had never made his religion an issue, and the Moslems who predominated had left him alone.

The bed was an old one, but it had an elaborate head and foot made of brass tubing. It still had an air of elegance about it, despite the discouraged droop of the mattress. The spread was a printed cloth with the face of one of the country's politicians – Tony studied it for a moment trying to remember if he'd ever met the figure who had been drawn on the cotton spread in large blue and brown strokes and set into a frame of vines and leaves. Then he sat down on the edge of the bed again, looking down at the light that flooded across the floor. He had brought the linoleum with him on one of his last trips up the river. He remembered when they'd put it down on the floors. He closed his eyes and leaned against the bed's brass frame, for a moment too filled with memories to get into his clothes.

There was a sound of footsteps in another part of the house. Albert or his wife would be in soon with breakfast. She always brought it for Albert to eat in his room, but her husband usually brought it in to guests. Tony hurriedly got into his shorts, put on his shirt, and with it still unbuttoned went over to the washstand in the corner of the room to splash some water on his face. He'd shave later. The washstand was the same age as the bed and it had the same air of another day's elegance. The water pitcher was chipped, but it was English china, and its pattern was as familiar to him as the other objects in the room. As he was drying his hands there was a knock at his door.

"Good morning, I have some breakfast for you." It was Albert's voice.

Tony opened the door. "Yes, it is a good morning. I haven't slept like this since I left."

Albert was carrying a plate instead of a bowl. He put it down on the table in the center of the room and took the cover off it, smiling self-consciously. "I know it won't be what you're used to, but my wife was able to find eggs and there is a little meat with it. I hope it will be satisfactory."

On the plate was a somewhat rumpled attempt to imitate an English breakfast. Tony shook his head. "No need for her to go to any bother, but give her my thanks." He held up his hands, "Didn't think I'd get an English breakfast this far from the old country."

Nindi was still in the sitting room when he finished his breakfast. She had made coffee and there were cups sitting on the table for the two men. "Lovely to see you all

63

again," Tony said. "Don't know when I slept so well. Woke with the birds. Just like the old days." He rubbed his hands together with a pleased expression. He didn't look as drawn as he had the day before, but there was still a paleness to his face, a tightness around his eyes. He had changed to a short-sleeved shirt, but he still had on his old uniform shorts. He'd put on sandals instead of the knee socks and his legs looked pale and defenseless, but stringy with muscle. He hadn't lost the strength in his legs, even if his shoulders and arms had become softer over the years.

"I hope the breakfast was satisfying. I couldn't get you all the things for a real English breakfast, but there were eggs."

"Delicious," he said, trying at the same time to think of some way that he could get the same meal of grain and honey that they ate. "Absolutely hit the spot. But I can do perfectly with the same fare you and Jabi – Albert – have. Don't think you have to go out of your way. It is appreciated, but just give me the usual rations."

"No," she protested, "At least we can give you a little feeling of home."

"Mustn't put yourself out. The least thing will do. I rather fancy the sort of thing you do yourself," he added with some uncertainty. "Don't feel you have to go to any trouble."

Albert came in from the porch and sat down at the table. "That is one habit which I got from you and it seems to stay with me even when all this time has passed."

"And that is?"

"I go out onto the porch every morning and I look to see what the weather promises to be for the day. But of course the weather never is any different. When it is the dry season it is always hot and when it is the rainy season it is always hot and wet. There isn't any change at all. You always had such an air about you when you went to the doorway and looked out with your hands behind your back. I admired it very much."

"I must have looked a bit of a fool at times."

"I didn't mean it that way," Albert said quickly. "I didn't

64

mean it that way at all. It is just that we noticed what you did because you were so new to us."

"You were as new to me. It was all so new at that time. Who would have thought it would all get so old – isn't that so, Albert – old before we noticed it."

Stanley Morrison, the young teacher, came into the room carrying his empty breakfast bowl. Hearing his footsteps Mrs. Jabi brought him his coffee. The night before he had come back to the house while the other men from the village were talking with their old District Officer. He was tall, as tall as Tony, but there was still a young gangliness to his body. He was wearing a light safari shirt over his trousers.

"Mr. Smythe, good morning to you. Albert, good morning." He sat with them and sipped from his cup. "I didn't think any of you would be up so early this morning. You were still all talking at the top of your voices when I went to bed."

"The birds," Tony answered. "Couldn't sleep a wink with all those twittering creatures about. Don't know how anyone puts up with it."

Albert lifted his slight shoulders, his eyes creased with amusement. "I think it has something to do with old habits. He was always one to be up before the rest of us to be sure we were out on our jobs."

"There was still talk of you, even when I came here four years ago."

"You can't have been here four years, Morrison, you don't look old enough to have been on the job more than six months on the outside." Tony found that the teacher looked so much younger than he expected and he was surprised at his own inability to judge.

"You are right, Mr. Smythe, I did come right from training school, but I was twenty then, and now you see me, twenty-four years old."

"I was thirty when I was posted here, and I supposed I

looked every day of it. Jabi here, he was eight years older than I was but I thought he was a boy. When he came to me and said he was the new school master I almost laughed at him, but I had to give him his due. He hadn't laughed at me when I said to him that I was the new District Officer; so I had to keep a straight face about it."

The three men laughed so noisily that Mr. Jabi's wife came to the doorway and looked into the room.

"Nindi, they've sent you a boy to take over your school. I wouldn't take his word for it when he tells you how old he is. Can't be a day over twenty."

"Oh, but he is, he is," she began earnestly. "I know that Stanley doesn't have a settled air about him, but he is more than twenty."

They began laughing again at her seriousness. "I suppose I'll have to accept that," Tony said after a moment and Nindi, nodding, went back to her kitchen.

"How many pupils do you have, Morrison?" Tony asked.

"Forty-five at the moment, though the number goes up and down over the term. I expect new arrivals to come at any time and I keep places open for any who do come."

"There were more pupils when you had the school, Albert."

"I had almost seventy for many years. But the number of children has fallen."

"We thought the village would grow, didn't we?" Tony was looking beyond them toward the window. He shrugged. "Don't let us keep you, Morrison. I know you have to get on with the job, but we'll have a chat in the evening." His tone had become almost self-consciously official. He had taken on so much of his old air of authority that the other man stood up immediately and nodded to them.

"I'll see you then," Morrison said, and nodding carefully went out onto the porch, down the steps and into the blinding glare of the trampled yard.

Since neither of them had anything to do Mr. Jabi insisted on bringing the chairs onto the verandah so they could sit and talk. He could get at his notes in the afternoon, there would be time to walk in an hour, before the day got too hot. At least for a time they could sit and not do anything at all.

Tony sat stiffly in the chair, one knee over the other, his arms crossed on his chest. To Albert he looked as quietly assured as he had when he'd been on his post. As though he were conscious of what the other man was thinking Tony nodded. "Feels a bit as though I should be getting back at the old job. You know, I haven't come to retirement age yet. If it hadn't been for Independence I'd be the D.O. here still."

"I didn't have the idea that you'd taken other employ-ment in England. In your letter you never told us of anything."

"Thought about it at the time. I was just fifty and a chap still has a lot left in him at that age, but the pension was enough for the two of us and it took us a bit of time to get the cottage put to rights and there was the garden as well, and then nothing that was offered tempted me."

"So your only employment was here?"

"I was only one of many, you know. There were a great many like me. I went to some of the meetings of the chaps who'd been in the Colonial Service. We tried to keep up some of our old ties. Some went into something else, but most of us just pottered about. Didn't seem worthwhile to begin anything new. We'd given it our best and then we'd been told we weren't wanted. That was that."

"At least you've come back to see what's become of your old job. It has been a little difficult – there have been ques-tions, you know, why you've come back."

"I should have thought that would all be clear," Tony said, surprised. "I hadn't paid a visit in donkey's years and it was time to see you all again."

"We are so grateful that you could come again, but it is so long to come only for a visit with us," Albert persisted, uncomfortable at his own questioning.

Tony looked off into the compound yard, at the sagging fence and the dusty leaves, at the long legged chickens strutting back and forth across the opening of the gate as they bent to peck at garbage the children had missed. "It is a long way. It was longer than I thought it would be to come back and then I waited so long, I had to do it alone. I didn't think I could do it without Beverly, but something told me I must, and when you hear a voice like that inside you all you can do is fall in line and carry on as best you know how.

"But it isn't as simple as that. I don't mean to say it was only something like hearing a little voice. It would take more than that to get me moving. But that came into it as well. Do you know I was homesick for the place, Albert?" he said incredulously, "I was homesick for all this. Christ knows it isn't much. It's a gaggle of huts pitched together in the back of nowhere – it doesn't have a building that wouldn't fall over in a good wind, there's nothing to look at except the trees and insects, it stinks to high heaven, and you spend half of your time here sick to death from some damned insect or other – but I was homesick for it."

He tried to laugh; then threw up his hands. "I didn't mean to run down the place," he went on after a moment, speaking with less animation. He looked down. "Don't know why I used the word homesick, except that England wasn't that to me when I got back. It wasn't home, somehow."

"But this wasn't home to you either. You said that to us many times."

"It seems I was mistaken," Tony said with sad irony.

"Then you are thinking of staying?" Albert was confused.

"No," Tony said after a pause. "I don't know if there's enough here to keep me occupied."

"But you had to come?"

"Yes, I had to come to the old place again, if only to have a chance to argue with you again." Tony tried to laugh.

"We didn't argue in the old days," Albert said gently.

"No, we didn't."

A few people passed along the pathway and they nodded to the two men on the verandah. They looked so incongruous together, the tall, white-haired, sunburned figure of Mr. Smythe, the short, dark-skinned, grizzled figure of Mr. Jabi, but they were comfortable with each other and the moments passed. "I am sorry to hear that you were homesick, as you say, for the village here, but whatever it is brought you back we must be thankful for it." Albert leaned back in the chair. Tony bent forward and began to tap one hand on his leg.

"I was homesick. Yes, I did say that, but it wasn't all so simple being back there. Other things came into it. I don't know if homesickness, or whatever it was, would have been enough to set me on my way just by itself."

"I wouldn't have thought it would weigh on you so heavily. You used to say often that you were homesick for England and that one more year here would absolutely finish you."

Tony stared across the yard. "I haven't been too well," he began suddenly. "Little something not quite doing its job down there. I spent a little time in hospital after the business with Beverly. But I had to come back one more time." He brought his hand down on his leg again. "You know, Albert, I'm not a stupid man."

Albert looked at him in surprise.

"No, I'm not stupid. I may have my limitations, we all do, and certainly I don't pretend that I knew every part of my job as well as I should have, but I'm not dense – things do get to me. Do you think I haven't heard what's said about chaps like me? I tried to keep up, you know, looking at magazines and listening to what the new chaps were saying about us, and I know what they called me. I was an imperialist, Albert. I was 'a corrupted manservant for a decaying empire,' as one chap put it, I was 'a running dog for international capitalism.'

"You always expect one or two to run down what you're doing, but I couldn't find anyone who had a good word to say about me. Not me in particular, but all the little fellows like me out in the bush doing their jobs and wondering why in piss all they'd taken the job in the first place. If I'd just got it back in England, from people who'd never been out to the Colonies and didn't understand anything – the bastards that were on us from the beginning – then I could have said, 'that's all mate, you can get off when the train slows down.' But I got it from here as well, from your side of it, from the chaps that had been here with us and seen the job we'd done. You don't expect praise for doing what you're supposed to, but I don't think I should have to put up with something like that."

He had become angry as he spoke. Albert stirred uncomfortably.

"But what is it you want to find here?"

"I thought I was doing one thing, and now I have people telling me what I was doing was something else. I had to know about it, Albert. It's no use sitting in a club arguing about it. Too many chaps wasting their time doing it. Whatever I did, I did it *here,* and this is the only place I can find out what it was, whether the job was what I thought, or what those others are trying to tell me. Then when I was taken sick I thought if I wanted to know anything, I'd best get on with it. A chap does want to know what he's done with his life, you know, Albert, even if it's all been some damned foolishness."

8.

They walked through the garbage strewn pathways of the village without speaking. At the beginning Tony had asked questions, but he had fallen silent. It was still early; the worst of the heat would come later. He had brought his old sun helmet with him, and he'd made Albert wait until he'd rummaged through his luggage to find it. In the last years some of the men he worked with had given up wearing their sun helmets and along the coast it hadn't been so imperative to have a hat on all the time, but even in his final months he'd always gone out with his head covered. The helmet, now yellowed and stained around the brim, was as incongruous as his baggy shorts. His appearance was so startling as he strode along beside Mr. Jabi that people who passed them stared at him in surprise. He looked so much like a figure from a period that most of them had forgotten, and his bearing, his abrupt gestures as he pointed out something, his eyes angrily peering out from under the hat's drooping brim, only added to his odd appearance. Albert, who was wearing an old shirt from his teaching days, looked at the things Tony pointed out with quiet resignation. He felt, himself, that he had somehow been wrenched back into his own past. He felt that both of them must look like cartoon figures from one of the drawings that had circulated before Independence, the lanky Englishman and the earnest African, with a large empty balloon drawn in the space over each of their heads, waiting to be filled with their speeches.

The speech didn't come until they'd almost reached the school. There was a store shuttered up – the owner was away from the village for the day – and under the roof that projected out over the street there was a dark square of shade. They stood in its shadow as Tony wiped off his face with his handkerchief. He was breathing with difficulty, but Albert couldn't tell if it was his anger or if he wasn't feeling well. Tony pushed the handkerchief back into his pocket. His hand was trembling.

"Not your fault for what I'm seeing," he began, still staring around him. "Don't know why I didn't see it yesterday, but I wasn't thinking too clearly. I'd just met my friends again and I wasn't looking around that much. But Albert, dammit, I must say damn it all, what has happened? You remember the days when we built the drains system. I peeled off my shirt and dug right along with everybody else for the first few days. We had it working. It was taking some of that garbage out of here. It hasn't been cleaned out in years and now the walls are collapsing. I mean – a man does a job and it becomes part of him – and I sweated over that drain. Every one of us did. And the pump. At least it's still working, but we dug a drain for that, too, that dumped into the main drains. I know we did because I dug along on that myself, just as I did on the other one. I sweated over it as well. I had a sore back and bloody fingers along with everybody else, but we did get it working. Now it sits in a sea of mud. The women must sink in it to their ankles when they go to fetch water. And the pathways! You could drive a cart down them and now you have to clamber up and down everything like a bloody goat. We had the garbage out of the village – we had the collection area and we got most of it burnt. But now it's strewn

72

everywhere you try to walk.

"I don't want to be hard, but – I know all I'm saying is damn it all – but what else can you do when you've seen something like this. The clock's been turned back! The old place wasn't this dirty when I finished. You could see that someone had laid it out, that it had some plan to it. Now it's falling to ruin. I don't know why it's happening. I don't know why it's falling down like this. There has to be a reason. There always has to be a reason. But I can't see what reason there could be for this."

"There have been some inadequacies in the new methods of repair," Albert said after a pause. He felt a stir of his old discomfort at criticism from Tony – from the District Officer – but he didn't feel any sting from it, despite Tony's obvious anger. "And people have moved away," he added tentatively.

"But it was to be something else, Albert. After Independence, when I'd gone, it was to bloom like a garden. I heard the talk, I read the papers that were passed around when no one thought I was noticing. Now – now – " he struggled for the words, "it's like locusts have come and picked it over. I don't know the people – I don't know this place." He had become more and more angry and he was breathing in uneven gasps, fanning himself with his hat. "This was home to me, Albert, home – as unlikely, as misjudged as it may seem, this was home to me. And look at it! What can a chap say about it?"

Albert realized for the first time that he was becoming old. Everything that Tony was saying was true, but he found that none of it seemed important to him. It would be someone else's concern. But he felt sorry for his friend.

"I don't think I am as conscious of it as you. That happens when you stay in one spot and become used to it. When I'm out on a trip and I stay in other places they are much like this."

"Have they all gone down so much?"

"Most of the villages had never come as far as this."

73

"I didn't know. I saw some changes on the coast. The city was bigger – it was almost modern; so I thought that here –. But I have to ask myself, 'What did I have to do with this? Would it have happened if I'd stayed on?' "

Albert stared at him. Tony had put his sun helmet on the back of his head and was wiping his flushed face with his handkerchief again.

"How could you have done anything about this?"

"At the end I might have let down without noticing it myself. I've thought about it. A chap does go to seed."

"But you did so much! It wouldn't be different now, no matter what you'd done."

Tony looked away, down the dirt street, staring at the shabby buildings and the litter of mango pits and donkey droppings on the pitted street. He took a deep breath, trying to calm himself. "Suppose it's my way of thinking. Chap begins to think of himself too much. I was here all those years, thought that perhaps I was having some effect, that I was getting a few ideas over. But I didn't cause much change. Can see it now." He jammed his handkerchief in his pocket with an abrupt gesture. Albert could see that he was still angry, despite his struggle to keep himself calm.

"But you did bring in improvements. It was different when you left from what it was when you first came."

"I wanted it to be a model, don't you know. Something to be looked up to. You work like bloody hell for something, you want to get something back for all your efforts, for all that you've put in."

Albert tried to think of some answer. He could see the unpainted boards of the shops, the streams of dust that drifted down the uneven walls, the refuse that had blown against the compound fences, the heaped garbage in the paths.

"I am sorry I must show you so much that disappoints you," he said finally.

"Isn't you," Tony responded, his mouth tightening. "Don't want you to think for a moment that I consider you part of all

74

this dirt and disorder. The only question I have is whether I might have been able to do something about it myself."

They walked again, saying little. At the end of the street they could see the gardens of the administrator's building. It had been Tony's office for most of the time he was there. It had been built during his first years on the post and he'd moved into it while the paint was still drying on the doorways and window sills. As they approached the office it was obvious that the garden was half tended and unkempt. The pathways hadn't been kept open, and the stones lining the flower beds had been kicked away. The little grass that was left in front of the flag pole was brown and withered. They went slowly across the garden and stopped in the shadows of the large trees that had been left in front of the building. The paint on the window sills had long since peeled away and the screens were torn and sagging where they'd pulled loose from the windows. The door to the office stood half open, but Tony hesitated.

"Don't want to push my way in." They could see the bench that was set against one wall for people waiting to see the Commissioner. It was newer, some of the wood still showing through the layers of grime that had already accumulated. There were papers on a desk just inside the door, but the room was empty. The only people they could see close to the building were two police constables with their uniform shirts hanging open, who had jacked up a car close to the side window and were stripping down the motor. Tony had always thought of the building and its garden as being the center of the activity that had surrounded him when he was in his office. The stillness dismayed him.

"The Commissioner is not in his office at this time of day," Albert explained, sensing what the other man was thinking.

"But this time of day . . ." Tony began, then stopped, sounding foolish even to himself.

"His hours in the office are irregular," Albert said

hurriedly. "It is only a part of his duties to be in the office seeing to schedules and petitions."

"When does a chap drop in on him?"

Albert was thoughtful. "It is usually better to send him your questions in writing, and in due time you will receive a response."

They stood in the shadows looking through the half opened door. Albert was more uncomfortable than he'd been at the beginning of their walk. He could understand a little of what the other man was feeling. He bowed his head and carefully smoothed the dust in front of one of his sandals. A tiny grasshopper desperately jumped away from his foot, in its headlong leap turning itself half over so that it landed in a clumsy heap under a clump of weeds. "You must understand, it is very different from place to place, just as it was in the Colonial period, when each district had its own pace of development."

Tony was staring at the door, one hand rubbing the back of the other, his mouth working impatiently. "Wouldn't do to go in without some kind of invitation. Wouldn't want someone to do it to me."

Abruptly he turned and strode off through the garden, going toward the path that led to the river landing. Albert hurried after him. Tony's thin body seemed to sway unsteadily as he came into the unkempt tangle of bushes at the bottom of the garden, but he veered off and when Albert came up beside him they could see the green surface of the river through the tattered brush. He finally slowed down when they had come to the bench under the eaves of the warehouse. He sat down heavily and wiped his face with his handkerchief. "Wanted to get a look at the river," he just managed to say, his breath coming in irregular heaves. Then he stood up again and shaded his eyes, looking in the direction of the water. Walking more slowly he went toward the pier and Albert again reluctantly followed him, not sure what Tony wanted of him. They stood on the oil-soaked planks jutting over the surface of the river and looked down at the

76

eddying current, at the iridescent green surface as the stream pushed past the logs supporting the planks. They could feel them trembling as the water pulled at the pier, as if dozens of hands were trying to push the pilings aside in their rush to the distant ocean.

Tony was still breathing heavily, slowly wiping the sweat from his forehead again.

"It's beginning to be hot," Albert suggested, trying not to show his concern. He glanced around him. If the heat were too much for Tony he would need someone to help with him. He could see a group of women washing clothes a short distance upstream. They would come if he needed help. It was difficult for Albert to think of something to say. He had expected Tony to laugh at the conditions in the village. He had thought he would shrug and think himself much better off not having to deal with all the problems. Albert had never been sure that he understood the other man, now he had no idea how to help him.

Just as abruptly Tony began walking again; this time back toward the village. With Albert hurrying after him as he strode ahead he turned at the row of dingy shops and plunged without hesitation into a dark opening at the end of a wall. He had come to the old market place, which hadn't been moved since he left. When Albert caught up with him he was standing silently at the head of an aisle, staring into the dimness while he waited for his eyes to adjust. He took off his sun helmet and wiped his forehead. The market was half empty, even though it was a regular day for people to come in from the surrounding areas with produce. He held the hat in front of him, studying the sweat band as though it had a message written on it. He jammed the hat on again and turned toward the opening to the street. "School next," he murmured as much to himself as to Albert, and he began walking again.

This time Albert let him go ahead. It was clear that Tony had decided to do one of his old inspection tours. Albert could see his ungainly figure in its old costume hurrying along the dirt pathway toward the school building. Albert waited in the shade for him to come back, reluctant as he always was to break into Mr. Morrison's classroom. The shop keeper in the doorway where he had stopped greeted him. As Albert knew he would he asked about Tony.

"That man, I believe, was the old D.O. here in the colonial days," the man said carefully, not sure what Mr. Jabi's attitude was toward the colonial days.

"Yes, he was," Albert answered noncommitally. He was reluctant to talk about his friend, but he found – to his own discomfort – that he didn't want this man to think that he would support anything Tony might say. He looked down the street, waiting for Tony to appear again.

"I didn't know him," the man went on after a pause, "but I heard about him and his digging along with the others for the drains. He was here many years, I understand."

"We came at the same time," Albert answered shortly.

"Then perhaps you could tell me what it is he is doing here with us again?"

Just then Tony's sloping hat brim appeared through a thicket of leaves. Albert started to follow him. Turning to the man he let himself smile ironically.

"I believe he is carrying out an inspection tour just at the moment." And he hurried out the door.

9.

Tony lay in his room resting until it was time to eat. He had gone from one end of the village to the other looking into huts and over fences and sliding down sand-banks to look for culverts and borders for the walkways and for stretches of wall and drainage pipes that Albert himself had forgotten about. It were as though a different village existed for each of them. Albert was always a few steps behind. He nodded to the people they passed, answering puzzled questions in a low voice, keeping an eye on Tony as he hurried on.

When Tony came out of his room again it was early afternoon. He nodded to Albert and his wife, who were in the sitting room waiting for him. Nindi stood up and started toward the kitchen. "You must sit and eat. It will be good for you."

Albert was watching him anxiously, but the mood of the morning seemed to have passed. Tony went slowly toward a chair and sat down. He pushed loose strands of his white hair over his ears and leaned back with a half smile. "Didn't mean to lead you such a chase, but once I'd started it didn't seem right to leave any of it out."

"I had forgotten so much myself. It was as though you had been here all the time and I was the one who had been away. It was most impressive to see."

Nindi brought in food. Again it was meat cooked with peppers in a bowl of rice, but this time she'd also cooked okra, the village's most common vegetable. As they ate Albert, who was still uncomfortably seeing so much of their lives as Tony was seeing it, felt the occasional tickle of goat hairs that had made their way into the okra. Almost anything cooked in the village had goat hairs in it, but he was so used to it he hadn't thought about it. Now Tony's obvious disapproval affected him as well, and he tried to fish the goat hairs out of his bowl and put them to one side without making it obvious what he was doing.

"Everything is still very hot," he offered as an explanation.

"After a chap's been away the food does take a bit of getting used to, but this is the way I always liked it." He laughed and shook his head. "Bloody goat hair and all, right Albert?"

They sat in silence after Nindi had taken the dishes away. They were drowsy, but neither of them wanted to sleep. Beyond the trees the sun had drained the sky of color and its blue tone was thin and streaked. Finally Tony broke the silence. "How long has the present Commissioner been on the post here?"

"Mr. Camara?" Albert looked up in surprise. "I must think for a moment. Several months, I would say."

"How many commissioners have there been since I left the post?"

"No one was like you, to stay as long as you did."

"Didn't have that much choice, but I do think I was fortunate and all to stay as long as I did. But how many would you say?"

"I'm sure I could find a list, but it has been a considerable number. Perhaps a dozen, perhaps fifteen."

80

"How can a chap get on with anything if he doesn't have some time on the job?" Tony burst out, some of the morning's anger coming back.

"It is difficult to get people to stay, Particularly if they are married. As you know, it is lonely here. I think it's harder for the wives than it is for the husbands since they have so little to do."

"Beverly was always busying herself with something."

Albert sat nervously across the table trying to find some way to answer him. He was thinking again of how often he had been uncomfortable at Tony's questioning. "Beverly was an unusual woman," he said after a pause.

Tony looked out over the glaring dust of the yard. He was clearly trying not to let himself become too upset. "Why did the others leave," he asked finally.

"Sometimes it was difficult fitting in. It became rather different when we had Africans taking over the post. I think we tended to watch them too closely. If the new commissioner was a man from a tribe that didn't have any contact with the people here then it sometimes became a problem with the language. None of them stayed long enough to learn the languages here and you remember how hard it was if you had only English to go by. Despite all my efforts at the school." He looked across at the other man and held up his hands. "There were also some instances of mismanagement."

"Of funds?"

"Of funds. And other things."

"That explains the ruin I see everywhere around me when I get outside the gate."

"That is part of it. But also it is a very poor country. It was always poor and it's hard to see how it will ever be any different. I think this is something that was not so well understood by younger men at the time when we were waiting for Independence."

Despite Mr. Jabi's concern at keeping his friend from becoming too upset, he could see that Mr. Smythe was still agitated. He was drumming on the table top with his fingers, his mouth set in a thin line as he stared in front of him without seeming to see anything. Albert was disturbed by their conversation. Tony had often been difficult in the past, and now he had become a little more trying. It was clear from the tone of the questions that his old friend was asking him to agree that it had been a mistake to dismiss him and the men like him from their posts. That it would have been better for the people in the village if they'd been kept on. That the new administrators hadn't been able to keep it all going without them. Sometimes Mr. Jabi had said these things himself in his own irritation at the slowness, at the shabbiness and the inefficiency, but he couldn't say them to Tony. He also couldn't be angry with his friend; since he did understand a little of his feelings. Almost in despair he tried to think of something to lighten the mood, hearing the drumming sound of Tony's fingers on the table top.

After a heavy silence they heard a new sound mingling with the afternoon's blend of bleatings and mooings and cluckings and the dull thudding of the wooden mortars as women pounded grain for the evening meal. It was the shriek of the children as they ran back to their own compounds as school finished for the day. In a few moments they would be joined by Mr. Morrison. Albert stood up and went toward the kitchen. "I must tell my wife that Stanley is on his way." His voice was light with relief.

They didn't hear Stanley's footsteps, but they could hear the murmur of greetings from the children and the women as the teacher came through the maze of paths back to the compound. It was like following the progress of a strange bird through a feeding area toward the end of the afternoon. Everyone had something to say to him. He was smiling when he turned in the gate and crossed the yard. His smile became even broader when he saw the two of them sitting at the table.

"Jabi, Mr. Smythe, it is nice to see you. Mr. Smythe, I must say, you made a hit in the classroom. I had many questions about you and about what you might be doing back in our village after so many years."

He sat down across the room from them and stretched out his legs. His manner was completely at ease, unlike the kind of tense regard Tony had felt so often from other people in the village. He wondered where Morrison had grown up.

"You're not from here?" he asked.

"My lord, no," Morrison laughed. "I was born on the coast of course, but I had a father who was in the Army and I spent a bit of time in England as a boy. Fact of it is I went back there for some of my training; then finished up at the school where Jabi did his training."

"Then they sent you here, away from all the bright lights and the excitement."

Morrison laughed easily. "It is a sleepy place, isn't it? I sometimes wonder myself how I stand it, but then along comes a good lesson from one of my pupils or a little picnic in the bush and I feel I can begin again. I won't be here too much longer – I think only to the end of this term. But I haven't minded it, don't you know. As they used to tell us in training school, somebody has to take up these posts."

"Or the job won't get done," Tony agreed firmly. "How right you are, Morrison. That's just what I told myself year after year while I stayed here and sweated away trying to make it go. Somebody has to do it or it just doesn't get done. That's what's happened here. No one's come along to see that the job gets done. I kept hanging on, telling myself if I don't do it nobody will, and now nobody is doing the job, Morrison."

Stanley shifted uncomfortably on his hard chair, confused by the vehemence of Mr. Smythe's outburst. Albert cleared his throat.

"We have just been taking a walk through the village and there is much that hasn't been kept in repair as it should be

83

and I'm afraid we have disappointed my friend in this regard," he explained to Morrison. "But I think we should all have tea," he hurried on, "I'll go see what I can do to help with it."

He went into the back of the house and the silence continued until he came into the room again. Tony was still drumming on the table and Morrison had leaned his chair back so he could look up at the ceiling.

"What kind of name is Morrison," Tony asked abruptly, a trace of irritation still in his voice. "It isn't African."

"It's English, of course," Morrison began, some of his usual cheerfulness coming back. "I am, however, not English, as you can see. I believe the name has something to do with slavery. I come from parents who were grandchildren of people who had been taken in the period of slavery. When they were freed all those years ago they took an English name, since their own name had no meaning to anyone. You could say that slavery still leaves its mark on me, even though I myself never knew anything about it."

It was Tony's turn to feel uncomfortable. He sat stiffly in his chair, absentmindedly running his fingers through his hair.

"Bit of a rum time for everyone, I would think," he responded after a moment's hesitation. "Wouldn't have wanted to be around when all that was going on."

They drank tea together in an awkward silence. Mr. Smythe seemed almost to have forgotten the other two and as he drank he stared down at the table. It was obvious he was still trying to control his anger. Finally he leaned toward Morrison.

"When we were on our little walk I couldn't help checking into this and that to see how everything was getting on. It wasn't what I expected it would be, Morrison, I don't have to tell you that. It's gone back. The place is in poorer shape than it was when I came here first as a green D.O. just getting his feet wet."

84

Stanley shifted uncomfortably. "Is this so, Jabi?"

"I must say it's true. I myself was here just at the beginning when Tony came and the condition of the village was better at that point than it is now, and with Tony here for so many years we added a great many more improvements."

"When Independence came I was only fourteen. Do you know when it came I really had no idea what it meant? You people had been here all of my life. Now I still don't understand that much about it. In training school we got all of what led up to Independence, but we didn't get a feeling of what it had all been like. At least not in places like this. So I'm afraid I don't know too much about what was done when you got out in the bush."

Tony stared into the distance, again not seeing anything. His eyes still were hard, his mouth set in a tight line. "It isn't only you who doesn't know much about it," he said in a half abstracted tone, as if he were talking to himself. "It isn't only you who doesn't know."

10.

For a moment Mr. Smythe hesitated, fussed with the buttons on his shirt. "Am I wrong, Jabi?"

Mr. Jabi looked surprised. "Wrong about what?"

"About the things I saw today."

"I think you saw them more clearly than I did, and perhaps in a different way than I did – but there have been changes. It isn't the way it was ten years ago."

Tony shook himself, snorting. "It's all so plain to see for you and me. All it took was one short inspection tour that only started to pull the covers back. I don't like to think about what's there if you really get your nose down to the ground and look close. But who knows it except chaps like you and me? Who will bring himself to say one word about it, when it's crying out to be said."

The other two men had no idea how to answer his outburst so they sat silently and waited to see what he'd say next.

"Morrison, you couldn't see what was happening and you live in the place. How could anyone else be expected to see it?"

"I think someone like myself needs a little time to see . . ." Stanley began, trying to find a conciliatory tone, but Tony broke in before he could finish.

"I don't hold you responsible, Morrison. Must make that clear. I do know what is said about chaps like me these days. I discussed it with Jabi, and as I said to him, I'm not stupid. I know all about what's said. No need to pretend, Morrison, I know you've heard it all. Men like me were bloody imperialists. That's what I mean when I say a man like you couldn't be expected to know what happened in a place like this. You get nothing but the same damned nonsense everywhere you turn.

"I think what it is that we're dealing with is that at the bottom of it there's something everyone would like to sweep under the carpet. Just what that is I'm sure Jabi could tell you as well as I can. What they're all trying to hide is the simple fact that we did so much. That without us there wouldn't be anything here. Isn't that so?"

He turned to look intently at Mr. Jabi, who was staring uneasily down at the floor. "When I came to the school here already a great deal had been accomplished," was the best he could manage.

"No, I don't mean to talk just about what you and I were able to do. I mean at the beginning, before you or I were on the scene. When all this business with a colony had just started. It was all foolishness what some chaps wrote, nothing here but cannibals and all that, but when the first fellow like me took up the post here the people round about lived like savages. There was still a bit of it when I came into it. Jabi, you must have seen much more of it when you grew up. Everybody without a stitch of clothes and as you can testify, Morrison, most of them slaves of one kind or other. If it hadn't been for us your grandfather or greatgrandfather – whatever he was – would still be a slave. Everybody here bloody sat and waited for us to come and put a stop to it."

Tony was becoming noisily agitated, tapping his fingers insistently on the top of the table as he talked, his voice slowly rising with the unresisting force of his anger.

"I know what's been said. I know what some people have said about how little we managed to accomplish, but I tell you – and it wouldn't be hard to prove – what we did was just a little short of miraculous. All this talk about how few roads we built, how few schools we opened up. How many roads were there in this God-forsaken bush when we came? Not one. There wasn't a school. There wasn't a church. And don't let anybody lead you up the garden path about the peace and harmony that existed here before we came. It was one war after another and it was one famine after another. There weren't even many people living here. Nowhere for them to settle with the wars going on all the time. That's what it was when the British came. Savagery. The only buildings were made out of mud and straw and sticks. You won't even see one of them today. The rains took care of anything that was old, that's how flimsy they were."

He managed to pull himself to a kind of stop and he looked from one to the other, still excited, but trying to hold back some of his feelings. "I don't think it's going too far to say that."

Stanley was looking at Albert Jabi, obviously waiting for him to say something. Some of this Jabi had already heard often before, but the tone had been different. Tony had never taken it seriously before.

"It is always so difficult to say what it could have been like before the colonial period. We have only certain tales and legends." Albert answered finally.

"I don't mean anything personal," Tony said quickly. "I don't want to say anything detrimental to anyone's past. Certainly no country's made a perfect job of it, though Britain's done better than most. But anything you see around you was put up after those first chaps had taken up their posts here. Everything – the roads you ride on, the building you're sitting in. I was here myself when the electricity lines finally were strung up to the trees and we set a little generator going to give light to a few of the houses. That's

88

what the job was – that's what you did. And that's what nobody wants to know about now. It doesn't look like much when you look around you and you think of how many people still live in the bush, but without the roads we built you couldn't even see that much. Do you know how many bridges I put in myself? Twenty-three. That's more than one a year. Doing the work with spades and some rusty hammers. I laid nearly a hundred miles of road. That last stretch when you come up from the coast – I did that with ten men from the village the last year I was on post. There was a late start to the rains and it gave us time to get the old footpath in some sort of order.

"Jabi – Jabi – " he broke off and held up his hands apologetically. "Don't mean to make such a hash of it. I used to have all of this at my fingertips, so to speak, but some of it slips away after a time. You try to do so much." He sat thinking, then lifted his head emphatically. "But the feelings are still there, no doubt about it. I know, Morrison, it can't look like much to you young people. Just a dirt road and a drainage ditch or two, but just look around. You take it for granted and it all begins to fall to pieces, just as it's doing here now.

"And Morrison – I looked at the lessons you had written down on the blackboard in the school. Every word was in English. You'd be out of a job without the language our chaps brought here. Jabi here would go without his pension. And I could see that the juju's still here. All those little pouches tied to the boys' arms. At least we made a start at rooting it out."

"I think what most of my pupils wear now is something written down from the Koran," Stanley interjected.

"Quite so," Tony responded triumphantly. "If we'd had time to finish the job we started, all of that would be gone now. If we'd been dealing with chaps like you two then all of it would be gone without a trace, but that wasn't the level we were dealing with. What kind of a system did they have here to set up the chief? No way of picking him, no way of sacking him if he couldn't do his job. I know it wasn't a real sort of democracy that I started here, and I used to feel sorry for that poor chap Suso when he had to come into the office with all those petitions, but it was a beginning. It wouldn't be too much to say it was the beginning of decency and civilization where there'd been nothing before.

"But Jabi can tell you this, Morrison. No need for me to bother you with all the details. Perhaps you know it as well as I do. You did go through the teacher's training program. It's not you who's saying those things. A chap would have to have the skin of an elephant to let it all slide off him. One beggar said the post was put up here to buy slaves, and nobody took him up on it. Nobody dared tell the truth. When the first District Officer set foot in the station here that had all been done away with for fifty years."

The rush of words slowed for a moment. His hands were trembling with the force of his temper. "I don't mean to blow my own trumpet. That was all done before my time. You know, Jabi . . . Albert . . . I don't ask for credit for my little part in it. It's all those other chaps I'm thinking of, the ones who did the job in the beginning. It's only justice to give them their due. Only simple justice before God and their fellow creatures.

"We only had sixty or so years here to do the job. That's all – but to hear some of those people carry on you'd think we'd been having our way out here for centuries. But that was all the time we had and, by George, our chaps made the most of it. So much was accomplished – it's the truth, Morrison, and Albert will tell you that we had nothing to do it with. Just our own stubborn belief that it could be done. I squeezed the last drop out of every shilling I managed to wangle out of those skinflints on the coast. You remember. Every shilling had to do the work of three. Digging myself, right along beside the men from the village. When I was out touring in the bush I made everybody keep the ceremonies down so we wouldn't waste time or money. Albert remembers. He was beside me on so many of

90

those meetings with the chiefs out there."

" 'Dig a well instead' was how you put it, I remember." Albert nodded his head.

"You must have had to put up with a lot of that ceremonial nonsense," Stanley rushed to add, hoping to be agreeable. "We try to keep it down in the school of course. The pupils have enough to do with their lessons."

Tony didn't seem to be conscious of their efforts to mollify him. He leaned across the table and tapped it for emphasis. "That's what I mean, Morrison. You have to keep a firm hand, or it all begins to run down. That was what we brought here – the British idea that a man has a job to do and the best thing for him to do, for himself and everyone about him, is to get on with it with no nonsense. Lord knows there was nothing in it for us. I think Suso did better with those extra rations you gave him when you set him up as chief than most of us did in the service. Oh, I grant you we had our house boys and all that, but we didn't have all the extra hands you have in your houses to help out, so we had to have someone to give us a lift with the housework.

"I don't complain, mind you. I was doing the job I wanted to do. But there wasn't anything in it except the satisfaction of a job well done. A chap had the sense of bringing a little light into the darkness."

He slumped back in the chair again. "I sound like one of those fellows who go about giving talks to retired officers' clubs. Don't mean it. Never could do the speeches part. Maybe that's why they left me out here all those years.

"But you know, Morrison," the fingers tapping the worn wood of the table top again, "it was hard on us, but it was even harder on the wives. Most stations you couldn't have a wife with you, and those girls were the lucky ones, the ones that couldn't come out here to these places. There were all the diseases and the lack of privacy and the appalling conditions. Sometimes when I was having a new latrine dug there wasn't anything for my wife to sit on. She might as well have gone out into the bush. Then when she did get sick all she could turn to for help was me and my medicine kit. I thought I'd lost her two or three times. If it hadn't been for Albert and his wife I would have lost her. They brought her in here and nursed her for a week until the fever went down. She couldn't follow me out on the tours so she had to be there in the house alone night after night, trying to keep up her morale by putting on a decent dress and sitting down to a table with candles on it, just as if I'd been there. But despite it all she went out in the village and worked beside me. She carried on when I was having my own tussles with fever. She got used to wearing mosquito boots and putting on her hat whenever she went out in the sun, she got used to ants on the floor and rats in the corners and goat hairs in the food. It did something to her. I could feel it, but she kept her chin up and she did her job. Nobody expects a statue for just doing his job, but there should be a medal for the wives and their way of sticking with it."

"It is a pity you had no chance to meet Beverly," Albert said to Stanley, trying again to change the direction of Tony's emotions. "She was an admirable woman. We felt close to her, almost as if she had come into our family."

"I am only sorry I didn't have the opportunity," Stanley said to Tony. He was relieved that the conversation was moving to less troubled ground, but at the same time he found that despite the older man's stale harangue he was drawn to him. He wondered if this was what had made the friendship possible with Mr. Jabi. What he could feel behind Mr. Smythe's anger was a hopeless idealism, a complete inability to fit into the world as it was. It was an idealism so completely part of the man that he didn't even see it in himself. It was, to him, something that had come with the post, like the letter tray or the mosquito net.

"Mind you," Tony continued after a moment, his voice lower, "you don't expect somebody to pay much notice to you at all for doing your job, but when I was mustered out I thought there'd be some notice of what we'd been doing here all those years. Outpost of the Empire and all that. But

92

nobody wanted to know. It was the 1960s and everybody was tired of hearing about the colonies, and they'd heard all those stories about the old days. You'd talk to a chap and he'd begin asking you about the pink gins on the verandah and the house full of servants and the wife in a bloody ball gown having a flirtation with the white hunter while her husband's off on a tour of his district. And you could tell that while he was asking you this he'd be seeing in his mind's eye all the pictures you got in the magazines of the black babies with their bellies swollen up to the size of a football because of hunger. The bloody same people who'd sent us out to be eaten up by the bloody mosquitoes didn't want to know about us at all. We were an embarrassment. After all that we'd given to this service—— and I knew chaps who died on their jobs – they wanted us to go off to a cottage in the country and potter in our gardens and not remind anybody of anything. Because we'd been in the colonies," Tony's voice was tired, the tone had become self-pitying, "we were treated like we'd come down with leprosy."

The three men sat in an awkward silence. Tony was sitting back in his chair, but he was still drumming on the table top with his fingers. Stanley stretched his legs and crossed one foot over the other. It was obvious that Mr. Jabi and Mr. Smythe had been friends because each of them had within him the same hopeless idealism, and it was just as obvious that each of them had made it possible for the other one to persist in his idealism with a tacit support that had gone unspoken all the years they had known each other. Stanley found himself starting to shake his head at them; then quickly looked away as Albert turned toward him.

"I don't know if anyone has told you," Mr. Jabi's voice was low and quiet, "but the two of us, Tony and myself, came to the village at just about the same time. We had to present our official papers to each other before we could say we'd settled into the post. I was different from you, Morrison, I didn't think that I would ever leave, as became the case. So my life here has been much like Mr. Smythe's life. We

93

worked side by side on many of the things that happened and for many years I had to help with the languages. We have so many here and it's no use to pretend that English will do for all cases. He did learn our basic language here, but there were the other languages as well. We had our adventures. I tell you I sometimes miss those days on tour when we didn't know what we would meet up with. We weren't in real danger, but it is true there were no roads and in the grass sometimes would be so many snakes."

He stood up and went to the door of his bedroom. "You must see a picture of us all in those days," and he went into the other room to take some of the photographs from the walls.

He spread the photographs out on the table, still in their painted window glass frames. Each of them saw the faces in the photos in different ways and each of them, for his own reasons, was silent over what he saw. Tony had with him only the picture of his wife that had been taken after they had returned to England, but in these photos she was still the timid young wife he'd brought out on post with him. Her face was so familiar, but at the same time he could see the mixture of vulnerability and determination he had described to the other two. She seemed so different from Albert's wife. As she stood next to the African woman, who was wearing flowing robes and a turban and layers of bracelets, her bush jacket and creased shorts and high boots made her look like she was wearing some kind of uncomfortable and inappropriate uniform. Her expression, as she stood staring into the camera, was more one of hope that she was doing what she was supposed to rather than any real conviction that she was succeeding at it. She had curled her hair for one of the photos. He could remember how she had struggled in the heat to set it, and then just as anxiously brushed it out, hoping that some of the curl would still be left when she had finished. He finally had to turn away, his eyes filling with tears that he was too embarrassed to show the other men.

94

Stanley looked at the two men in the photos. The slight, anxiously smiling figure of Jabi looking up at the large figure of Smythe. Jabi's face seemed even darker skinned in the prints, his expression young and concerned. Beside him Tony smiled broadly, his skin still as white as it had been when he left England. They looked almost shy of each other, the small, dark African and the tall, pale Englishman, but at the same time they were standing side by side, their shoulders touching, and they were smiling together at the same thing. It was obvious from the photos that despite their incongruities the two men were friends.

The pictures were much more familiar for Mr. Jabi, but he saw again how beautiful his wife had been then, and he felt a new warmth toward the image in the photo. They had all been so young – and in their own way they were still somehow young. He smiled back at the faces behind the glass as he stood at the table looking down at them.

Steps on the porch interrupted them. Tony surreptitiously wiped his eyes and turned toward the open door. A woman was standing outside. She was young – in her mid-twenties, he thought, and though she was African she was dressed in European clothes, a light colored blouse and a slim skirt that came below the knee. She was a handsome woman, tall and slender, but she seemed unsure of herself, standing in the doorway waiting for someone to notice her. When they turned around there was an awkward pause.

"Hello, hello," Morrison said finally, breaking the silence. She stepped inside. "How do you do, Morrison, how do you do, Jabi."

Albert took her hand and led her toward the other side of the table where Tony was standing. He smiled as he brought her forward. "Hello," he was saying to her and nodding toward Tony. "I would like you to meet someone of importance in the village. This is Mrs. Camara. It is her husband who is the District Commissioner."

95

Tony was surprised. He hadn't expected that the Commissioner would have a wife, after the things Albert had said about the difficulty of getting someone to stay on the post. Mrs. Camara looked too carefully dressed to be spending her life in a small, poor village hundreds of miles in the bush. She took his hand nervously. She didn't seem to have the kind of self-assurance he'd expected.

"I would have known it was you." She was half looking toward him, speaking in a low voice. "There were still some pictures of you when my husband took over the office. It is my husband who sent me over on my errand. I am to ask you to pay us a visit later in the day. He said I was to ask you over for a 'sundowner' and you would know what he meant."

"It was the first drink of the evening. It wasn't considered good form to drink before the sun went down. I haven't heard the term for years." He laughed and turned toward Albert. "Do you remember it?"

"I only heard it used when you had visitors. Since we didn't ever drink here you didn't use it with us."

"I believe it is something my husband found in one of his books," she murmured apologetically.

"Which of his books could it be in?" Stanley asked.

"I don't mean one of his own books." She was becoming more flustered. "He has been reading a number of books about the colonial period," she added lamely.

"That would certainly be me," Tony said briskly, trying to help her. "The term would also be from my time. Don't know if it's from yours at all."

"Oh no – but Stanley ... Mr. Morrison," she corrected herself, "might perhaps have heard it."

"I think that was all past when I got back here. I was too young. Just as you. We were both of us too young to hear all the talk." Stanley smiled at her as he spoke.

"My father had so many visitors at the end – just before Independence – I can remember sitting upstairs and hearing the voices. There was someone to see us almost every evening."

96

Her voice changed when she spoke to the school teacher, and she broke off, as if she were suddenly conscious of it.

"Was that just at the end? Just before the flag was lowered and all the rest?" Tony's voice was ironic.

"Yes."

"I didn't have any visitors at the end. Only Jabi here, and he had to do his duty whether he wanted to or not. Not a one came by in those last weeks. However it was all a long time ago. So long ago it's hardly worth remembering. It must have been exciting for you."

"I only remember a little."

"I have been listening to the two of them go on," Stanley said, nodding toward the other men. "I think they remember everything that happened here, between the two of them. It is a pity you weren't here to listen to all of it."

"Not at all," Tony interjected. "If we'd had a lady in the room we would have talked of something else."

"I find the village women don't stay in the room when the men begin to talk," she answered. "Do you mean it in that way?"

She was becoming less uncomfortable with him and Tony found himself responding to her. "No," he smiled, "most of our wives took a walk when the talk turned to business. Just plain and simple boredom."

"Was it boring?" she asked. "Boring for them?"

He turned and looked at her sharply. "No, it wasn't boring for them – just the opposite, I'd say." His tone was defensive. "But they had to put up with too much talk from us about the job. Are you bored here?"

She became flustered and took a step backward. "I don't . . . no, I don't think . . . ."

"Sorry. Didn't mean to strike so close to home."

"She has found certain things to do . . ." Stanley began, but Tony waved him silent.

"I know too well how it is for a woman out here. Not an easy job at the best and this place doesn't make it any easier. Isn't that so?"

97

Completely confused by this point she began backing toward the door. "I must get back. But you others," she looked toward Stanley and Mr. Jabi. "Will you come as well? My husband hopes to see you all. He would appreciate it if you could come together and give us a little chance to talk." She looked from one to the other appealingly.

"I'll have to make myself presentable, so it won't be quite at sundown, but you can expect me," Tony answered, "and I imagine you'll see the other two as well."

As abruptly as she'd come she shook hands and left them. They watched her cross the dusty compound, her tall body swaying slightly as she walked, the European clothes emphasising her tight waist and hips in a way that the loose robes the other women wore only concealed. Tony held up his hands. "Didn't mean to get after her that way. Don't know how I got started. Haven't been around women enough in the last months."

"I don't think she was upset by it," Stanley said.

"She could have sent a boy with the message," Tony continued after a pause. "No need for her to go across the village to deliver an invitation."

"She has paid us visits from time to time," Albert answered carefully. "I am pleased to think she considers us as friends."

"What about the husband?"

Stanley and Mr. Jabi exchanged a glance, then realizing that Tony hadn't noticed anything Albert shook his head. "Her husband is a busy man and he doesn't often honor us with a visit, and then it is not usually at the same time as his wife."

11.

They walked slowly in the darkness, picking their way over the rubbish and the water-filled ditches as they went across the village to the Commissioner's residence. Stanley had brought a flashlight, and he walked in front to light up the worst places in the path. The village was filled with the desultory murmur of people talking after supper, with the noises of the animals, the sounds of the last birds settling into the trees for the night. There was a persistent undertone of radios, all of them tuned to the same government station so that the voice of the evening news service took on an echoing aura of importance. The sounds seemed out of place in the darkness. As they came past the gates of the compounds they could see the low yellow gleam of kerosene lanterns in most of the huts. There was some electricity in the village, but it still hadn't made its way much beyond the official buildings, the Commissioner's residence, and a few of the corner stalls. The light streamed from the stalls out onto the shadowed pathways. The spaces were lit with bare bulbs and most of the stalls had no fronts – only a counter set back under a sloping roof; so the glare flowed out from the front to the dark forms of the shadowed huts. Under the glare was the usual jumble of trade goods – canned fruit, bars of soap, cigarettes, matches, lantern wicks.

"What about this Camara chap," Tony said in a low voice to Mr. Jabi after they'd reached the street leading to the Commissioner's residence.

"What do you mean?"

"What sort of a job does he do – what's the community think of him? Things like that."

"I must say the community thinks rather highly of him. He is a very ambitious man and he has brought considerable attention to the village."

"Not by the work he's done around the place," Tony said with a shrug of dismissal.

"No, that is very obvious, but it is in other areas that he has been the most active. He is quite highly regarded as a commentator on the political situation and has written a number of articles which have been placed in newspapers not only here but in the other of the old English colonies to the south. There is talk of a book being gathered from them and there is also talk of a government publication of some of his thoughts. He is a most clever man."

"How is he ambitious?"

"I think I would say that it is in the political sphere that his ambitions lie, though I wouldn't presume to know what it is he is planning," Albert said with his usual care. "One of the difficulties for Mr. Camara is that he must be away from the village so much. As you yourself said, it is a small place. Not really a sphere of action for a man who wants to do something larger. So he must be on the coast a good deal."

Tony was walking slowly over the broken stones and heaped litter, the light from the flashlight elongating the shadow of his legs so that he seemed to be striding over the ground with a spider's bent scuttle. "If he's as ambitious as that I would think he'd want to stay put, do the job he's supposed to do."

"I will say for Mr. Camara that he is a man of ideas and of

100

general principles, and he is of the opinion that if his ideas succeed on the larger scale then the country will be changed over, and with it all the villages like ours."

"A chap can lose himself in that kind of dreaming," Tony answered shortly.

"As I said, Mr. Camara is very ambitious."

The Commissioner's residence had been renovated and painted since Tony had lived in it, but it was still so familiar that he stopped at the steps and looked up to the porch and the windows and the hanging shutters. It was a low stucco building with a porch running the length of the house along one side. The shutters had been painted a dark green when he lived in the house, but now they had been painted the same white color as the plaster of the walls. The porch was deep – he had built it so that there was shade during the day. As he stood staring up at it he had the momentary apprehension that the old residence had become like the half opened door to his former office. It was open to him, but it was closed to him. He was welcome into the rooms, but not into the place that the rooms represented.

His memory of the house, of the porch, of the walls themselves was still strong enough that he hesitated for the sake of the memory. He realized with a kind of despair that to come into the rooms again, to walk through the hallways and look in the doorways – changed and altered now – would somehow disturb the memories he had of his own presence there. That early memory, like a half-glimpsed, evanescent scene, of himself there, of his wife, of the two of them together in those rooms, was so precious to him that he turned to go when he reached the first step. For a moment he was ready to leave without looking again at something he'd built so long ago.

But as he took a breath, his foot on the step, he found that his first notion wasn't strong enough to overcome his curiosity. He wanted to see what the place looked like again, and he told himself that he would find it so changed that his first memories of their life there would be left undisturbed. He had, however, no chance to make any decision at all. Mr. Camara had heard them as they came up the concrete of the walk and stepped through the doorway holding out his hand and greeting them effusively.

"Mr. Smythe, it must be. Jabi, hello. Hello, Morrison. Come in and make yourself welcome in our residence, which I believe for some time was your residence, Mr. Smythe?"

"Yes, yes," Tony answered, advancing up the stairs. "It's the old place. I didn't know until I thought about it on the journey, but I was settled in here longer than any place I lived since I was a child." He was shaking the Commissioner's hand, but he was looking past him into the hallway and he was talking almost to himself. The old wooden rack for hats and coats was still behind the door. He had built it himself, not expecting that it would last more than a year or two, and here it was still on the wall ten, fifteen years later. He stopped for a moment, looking closely at it. "Trying to remember. Put that up as well, but can't remember when I did it," he said finally, again as much to himself as to anyone else.

The Commissioner's wife had come to the door and stood waiting for them. She had put on a more elaborate dress, but her hands were squeezed nervously together at her waist and she seemed as unsure of herself as she had been in the afternoon.

"Hello, hello," Tony called to her. "Hope we didn't keep you waiting too long."

"No. I think that anytime after sundown would be alright.' She shook his hand, greeted the other two and led them inside.

The rest of the hallway and the room she brought them to had been changed many times since he had lived in them, but the walls, the dimensions, the character of the rooms – it was all still there under the new paint and the slight altera-

102

tions that new tenants had made. He went ahead into the sitting room and slowly walked around. The others sat and waited for him to finish looking. It was a high-ceilinged room, square in shape. There was a window in one wall opening out onto the porch, and there were doors that led to the hallway and the dining room. The furniture was in the old veneer style he remembered so well, even though the sofa and the chairs were new. Everyone who had lived in the quarters had left something behind, so that the room had a cluttered appearance, but at the same time it was without any special character – like a hotel in a small city or like one of the innumerable guest houses he had stayed in when he traveled to other districts. There were lamps on the tables, but they didn't fully light up the room, and there were dark spaces along the ceiling and in the corners.

"This room must hold many memories for you, Mr. Smythe. I believe that the residence was completed in 1953, which would mean that you made this your home for twelve years."

The new Commissioner was making an effort to be bluff and hearty.

"It could have been twelve years," Mr. Smythe conceded. "Don't have records of everything myself, left it all for the chap who took over." He had pulled up one of the chairs and was sitting stiffly, one leg crossed over the other, his arms folded on his chest.

"We have promised Mr. Smythe his sundowner," Camara's wife broke in. "Will it be whiskey?"

"Wouldn't want to drink alone – anyone else?"

"I'll have something," Camara said. He looked questioningly over at Mr. Jabi and Mr. Morrison, who were sitting back in their chairs watching the two men with some apprehension.

"Thank you, squash will be fine," Albert said and nodded his head.

Morrison nodded with him. "I believe I'll have a whiskey myself. What's it called, a sundowner?"

"Haven't heard the term for years," Tony said.

"Perhaps that is so," Camara answered pleasantly, smoothing his shirt down over his stomach, "I have been reading in your colonial literature and found the term there. Quite good, I thought."

"I didn't know we had a colonial literature," Tony murmured.

"One must admit that it is not extensive, but it exists nevertheless. A number of novels are of interest – some pamphlets as well, introductory materials to a tour on station, and so forth. I found also a cookery book which said that for no reason should the new District Officer endanger his stomach by eating the same foods as the natives. One can read a great deal into the material that is there."

"Didn't have time to read when I was on the job. If the ship didn't get up the river we didn't even have the papers to see what the news was in the rest of the world. Gibraltar could have sunk into the sea without our knowing until the ship made its way up to us."

The new Commissioner nodded. "As I was reading I did get the impression that those of you stationed so deep in the bush did get a bit out of touch."

It was evident to everyone in the room that he had said the wrong thing, but no one was sure whether or not he'd done it on purpose. He had leaned back in his chair and was still smiling, his eyes on Tony's face. In an effort to avoid the confrontation between the two men Albert hurriedly interrupted.

"I was also here in the village during much of this time and I must say that we felt ourselves so occupied here we didn't have a chance to think beyond our jobs."

"No," Tony broke in, and they waited for him to continue in an edgy silence, "I don't want anyone to think that we weren't in touch. Any one of us was always in touch with what was happening, even if we didn't make a fuss about it. The thing was to know why you were here and what you were doing. A chap had his job to do and he just got on with

104

it. Didn't make all that difference what they had to say at headquarters. Some of them there didn't have any idea what we were doing out here, what we had to put up with. Mind you, they had their heads on straight when it came to the big questions. They had that all sorted out."

"So you did have a feeling of isolation?" the new Commissioner asked, watching the other man carefully.

"I wouldn't say that we ever felt we were isolated," Tony said evenly. "You might have read somewhere that someone felt himself left out a bit when he was off in the bush, but that was all just wind up on our side. No one in the Colonial Service had any reason to feel isolated. The chaps in it with us were first rate, knew their jobs, and the best way for them to do their job was to let us alone to get on with ours."

"And what did you consider your job to be?" Camara asked slowly.

"To bring civilization here," Tony answered loudly, "to bring civilization to a part of the world where there had never been a sign of it before."

In the silence that followed Tony's pronouncement the Commissioner's wife brought in the drinks. Tony stared down at his glass, feeling suddenly uncomfortable in the room, even if he still thought of it as somehow his. Mr. Camara sat a moment; then raised his glass. "Is there a toast you would like to propose? Something from the old days? From what I could determine in your books the usual toast was to the King."

Tony shrugged. "It seems a bit remote now."

"Then I think it only fitting that we drink to you, Mr. Smythe. Whatever happened in the past you spent many years of your life here in this village and there are many old friends," he nodded toward Mr. Jabi, "who welcome you back most heartily. So I propose the toast to you, to welcome you on your long awaited return."

The others murmured and nodded, holding up their glasses. Tony didn't know how to react. It was like a scene out of some book he'd read when he was a schoolboy. He tried to remember what the hero had done in response to it all. As he sat looking down into his drink Mr. Jabi, on a sudden impulse, stood up and after a momentary confusion Stanley Morrison stood up beside him. They nodded to Mr. Smythe as he sat flustered in his chair. Mr. Camara didn't rise. He sat holding his glass, sipping politely when they toasted Mr. Smythe, his eyes going from one face to the other. He shifted his heavy body in his chair and casually arranged the sleeves of his shirt. With a flourish the two men sat down again as they tried to pick up the conversation.

Camara leaned toward Mr. Smythe. "You were here for twenty years, Smythe. I was looking through the old records. I know that it was not unusual for one of you people to have more than one or two years on the same post, but I never heard of anyone left in one spot for so long."

Tony shifted uncomfortably. He suddenly felt himself an object of curiosity. The comfortable pond of understanding he had with the other two men had evaporated and he was left dry on the beach for this unfamiliar creature to pick at him. He sat up in the chair and recrossed his legs.

"I'm sure the people who made up our assignments knew what they were about."

"Oh, I don't doubt it, but it still must have seemed a little odd to you."

"It didn't occur to me to question their judgement. I think I rather felt just the opposite. The work we had to do here needed many years to see it through. I would have stayed on longer. I think many of us felt the same way."

"You weren't ready to leave when the job was up?" Camara asked in a sharp tone.

"No – most of us were ready to continue. It wasn't a job to us. No," Tony's voice had also risen. "We didn't think of it as a job at all. To us it was a responsibility. A chap begins to feel that when he's worked in a place for a time. If you stay on

106

here you might begin to feel a little of it yourself. There were others like me who had several years on the post. We wouldn't have left if the decision had been made by us. That was all done over our heads. If the truth were known most of the people we worked with, the Africans, felt the same way we did. They couldn't say anything, what with the excitement over the new flag and the singing and all that, but they also wanted us to stay on."

"Did you ask them?" Mr. Camara said drily.

Again the room was still, but the silence was a stiff presence around them. It was obvious, this time, that the Commissioner had said exactly what he wanted to say. Tony was staring down at his drink, his mouth working, when there was a sound on the steps and someone knocked on the outside door. The Commissioner gestured impatiently for his wife to see who had come. He waited with an annoyed expression, tapping his heel against the leg of his chair. When his wife came back into the room with an old man in carefully washed but faded trousers and a much mended shirt he started to wave the man away, but Tony had already stood up and crossed to him. They took each other by the hand and began talking excitedly. Jabi, looking excited, leaned toward Mr. Camara.

"It is one of the house boys who served Mrs. Smythe. I didn't know any of their servants still lived nearby."

The door opened again and two small boys, who had obviously come with the man, edged into the room looking apprehensively around them. The Commissioner tapped his heel against his chair again, one hand marking a cadence on his knee.

"What are you two saying, Mr. Smythe," he called out abruptly.

Tony half turned toward him, the other man taking a step away, clearly frightened by the tone of the Commissioner's voice.

107

"We're simply saying hello to each other. This is the local language, Mr. Camara, I would have thought the Commissioner would make it his business to learn it."

Mr. Camara's heavy face began to swell and his heel stopped its tapping.

"There are at least four local languages, Mr. Smythe, and no one who has been on the post for so short a time could be expected to learn them."

There was another strained silence. "He was one of the boys who served my wife during the last years of our stay," Tony said finally. "Just learned I was back and he came by to pay his respects."

The two began talking again, Tony standing with his back turned toward the Commissioner.

"But why did he come here to the Commissioner's Residence to find you? Did he think you'd come back to take over your old post again?"

Tony had begun breathing heavily, and he had to pause a moment to get his breath before he responded. "He went first to Jabi's, of course. Was told he'd find me here." Tony took an unsteady step toward a chair and leaned on the back of it. His face had grown paler and he held one hand clutched against his side.

Camara looked uneasily up into Tony's face. "Does the man speak English, Mr. Smythe? If he does perhaps he could join us for a few minutes."

Tony struggled to catch his breath. "Not at my best at the moment. Have to forgive me." After a moment he turned and spoke to the older man. Across the room Albert said something to them, also speaking the local language. He stood up, nodding uncomfortably at Mr. Camara and going toward the other two at the end of the room. As they stood talking together Mr. Camara became more and more impatient, his tapping heel making an ostentatious comment on the interruption. Albert turned to him, holding one hand on his friend's arm.

"It's been a hard day for Mr. Smythe." He was anxiously

trying to explain the situation to the annoyed Commissioner. "He isn't yet used to the food and I believe he had too much sun. You have to expect little difficulties of this nature when someone's just come back into the heat here." He and Tony talked again, then said something to the older man, who nodded nervously to the others in the room, took the children by the hand and went outside. Tony stood for a moment beside the table, then walking with slow care made his way back to his chair. He lifted his drink and sipped from it, his hand shaking as he put the glass back on the table beside him.

"Told him to go on and wait for us back at Jabi's. He was a good chap, loyal as they come."

Camara cleared his throat in his irritation. "Perhaps you would like to rest and we can postpone our visit until another time. Though we have our duties to perform there is always the odd moment when we can fit in a visit."

Tony shook his head, straightening his shoulders. His breathing was less labored and Albert went back to his own chair. "Be better in a minute. Just have to catch my breath."

They all sat waiting until he was more composed. Mr. Jabi smoothed his hands on his trousers. "Mr. Smythe wanted to walk about the village to see the old sights today, and even though it was early and he had on his sun helmet I don't think it was wise."

"I was informed that you had a look at what we are attempting to do here. What would you say is the look of the place after so long a time?" In his anger Mr. Camara had become coldly precise and polite.

Tony lifted his head and said something half intelligible, but before he could finish he abruptly tilted forward in the chair and slid to the floor, trying to hold himself up with a shaking arm before finally sprawling on his side in front of them, his lips moving. As Mr. Jabi jumped up to try to keep him from falling he realized that the word his old friend was trying to say was "pigsty".

12.

It was decided that Mr. Jabi would help Tony back to his compound, even though Tony insisted that it was only a momentary fainting spell and that he would be able to continue after a few moments rest. The Commissioner and his wife went with them to the door, then came back into the room and he sat down noisily in his chair. He had asked Mr. Morrison to wait and finish his drink, but Stanley stood up and started toward the door.

"I think it would be better if I went along as well."

The Commissioner waved his hand in an abrupt gesture, which Stanley interpreted to mean he was expected to stay. The Commissioner's wife had gone back to the sofa and was looking down at the coffee table, running her finger up and down the side of her glass, leaving lines in the condensed moisture that had collected on it. She seemed undecided about whether she should stay in the room with the two men or if she should leave and go back to her quarters.

"No," her husband said to Stanley. "No, Morrison. We don't need to give up the entire evening, just because one of our party is indisposed." The Commissioner settled down

110

into his chair. "How is your drink?"

"I never had time to drink it." Smiling, Stanley held up his glass and took a sip from it, but at the same time looking over the edge of the glass at the woman who was sitting without moving on the sofa.

"Were you there today?" The Commissioner asked, trying to appear light and relaxed.

"Was I there for what?" Stanley answered, confused.

"For our Mr. Smythe's informal inspection tour, which I have heard so much about in the last few hours."

"Not from Tony."

"Of course not from Smythe. From everyone else here. The man didn't have the decency to tell me what he was about. Something could have been arranged for him. Instead he went off on his own, without anyone from my office to guide him."

Stanley looked down at his drink and tried to think of something to say.

"I had the impression that he didn't need someone to guide him. The place is much like it was when he left it. At least that was his comment."

"Then you were with him when he made his walk about!" It was obvious that Camara was still upset after his abortive meeting with Mr. Smythe. He leaned toward Stanley, waiting for him to say something, one hand fisted and pressed against his thigh.

"It isn't true that I was with him, but he did pay us a visit at the school. He had helped put up the building, he told the pupils. They were quite taken with him."

"Do I understand you to say that you permitted him to speak to the classes?"

Stanley put his glass on the table, rested his hands on his knees and looked across the room at the Commissioner.

"I didn't, as you say, permit him," he answered gently. "The truth of it is I asked him if he would like to speak a few words to the pupils since he had built the school building and so forth. Also, as I am sure you are aware, many of our younger pupils have not seen a white man except in their books and none of them has seen someone who represents that class of colonial officer we have read of in our history classes. I was of the opinion that this could not be harmful to my pupils. I thought it would be an experience they would benefit from."

"What language did he speak in?"

"He was very good, really. He must have had a great deal of experience speaking with groups when he was on post here. He spoke a little in all of the languages the children knew, as well as commenting on everything in English so they could practise their lessons. There were many jokes. I laughed myself at some of the things he said."

"Where were you brought up, Morrison?" Camara asked.

"On the coast, of course, though I was in England for a bit of my childhood and then I was there for some time again when I was in training."

"Then you know rather little about life as it was lived here in the bush."

"Like everyone else we still have relatives who live in rather isolated villages and there were visits when I was a boy – but I didn't really come to know the bush until I found myself in the village here."

"How does it happen that you have an English name?"

Stanley shrugged. "It has been in the family now for many generations."

"You enjoyed your time in England?"

"It was not so pokey as it is here. You can learn a lot living in a large city with all different types of people."

"You had no trouble with people because of your color?"

"Small slights, nothing more than that, though I was careful to stay out of a situation where I wasn't wanted."

"Small slights! Think of it, you have lost your own name due to the English and their slavery, I presume you are a Christian, so you have lost your religion. Here in Africa people were deprived of their lands and their way of life, and there in England you must walk a careful line to avoid

112

trouble because of your color. I would call these more than small slights."

"The things that happened to me I saw only as small slights, and they came from people I didn't need to respect."

"Morrison!" Camara exclaimed in exasperation. "There is no need for you to respect anyone, unless that man has earned your respect."

"You're too hard on him," Camara's wife protested.

"No, I'm not hard enough," he insisted. "Morrison, I have been engaged in a number of projects since coming here and you and I have had little opportunity to talk. It isn't only the education I received that has formed the opinions I hold. You don't know how I grew up, you don't know what I experienced. I grew up in a village not much larger than this one."

"I think everyone has read your articles," Stanley said, trying to lighten Camara's mood, just as he had done with Smythe in the afternoon.

"What the articles don't say is that the village was like this one, it had a resident District Commissioner. The man didn't leave his post until Independence, when I was in my teens. I grew up seeing the system, I knew who these men were and what they did. I heard from the moment I was a child that they brought us civilization. You heard it from Smythe again tonight. I don't deny that from the technological point of view we were very far behind when the first colonialists came. Our civilization had been built to different ends and to different purposes. We respected the family. I couldn't see that they respected anything. When the war came what could they tell us then about their civilization? In our wars at least we could kill only so many with our arrows and spears.

"They will tell you we had no roads, no schools, no machines. I grant you we didn't have these things – but once we had seen them we could have made them for ourselves. Whatever the colonialists did we could have done ourselves with more speed and more justice. They said they were bringing progress to us – for their own advantage they were

113

preventing us from creating progress ourselves. They gave us no industry, they only took our materials, they gave us a little education, but only enough so that we could do menial jobs for them. I know what they say, they built so and so many hundreds of miles of roads, they opened so many schools, they did this and they did something else. I'm sure if you talk to Smythe he will tell you all of these things. What they don't say is that we did the work, it was our hands and our bodies, and if they hadn't been in our way we could have done the job much better. Have you considered that, Morrison? Have you thought about it in those terms?"

As Mr. Camara began to sound more and more like one of his articles Stanley felt himself hemmed in somewhere between the two men – Smythe who had harangued him this afternoon, and Camara who was using him to listen again to his own opinions this evening. Stanley shifted his legs, stretched them out in front of him and looked down at his feet. He knew Camara would go on talking whether he said anything or not. He thought wryly that it was almost as though the two men were mirroring each other, only in a kind of mirror that reversed everything it saw. As the two of them held up their mirrors in front of each other they got only continually echoing images of their own attitudes.

"I know you don't read the statistics, but everything has gone on since Independence. The world here didn't stop just because Mr. Smythe and the others like him packed up their mosquito repellent and went home. We have gone on building roads and we have gone on opening schools, even if the press in their part of the world doesn't notice what it is we're doing here."

"You mustn't let Smythe irritate you," Stanley said mildly, looking across the room and smiling at the Commissioner's wife, who was still watching them anxiously.

"It isn't Smythe, Morrison, it's a whole system, it's a whole way of thinking. It was economic servitude that was imposed on us, that was imposed on the world they controlled. I cannot accept that. I cannot accept that any more than I can

114

accept the insult to our culture and history. They considered us little more than savages, and if there was something in our system that didn't agree with theirs they tried to do away with it. Their assumption always was that the British way was better, and that they could impose on us whatever system they saw fit. I don't deny that it is useful to learn English. It is a world language and someone who is ambitious had better learn a world language if he wants to make a career. You know that yourself, since you have traveled, you have been out in the world. It would do no good to speak one of our own languages. But at the same time it was an insult to push our languages to one side, to let them languish. This was the language of our forefathers, it was the language of our culture, it was our history and our code of law and conduct. To try to push it aside was to push aside our lives."

"You've written these things in several of your articles," his wife said hesitantly. "I don't think Stanley disagrees with you."

"Stanley?" he looked at her confused for a moment. "Oh – Morrison. No, these things can't be said enough."

The Commissioner was sitting forward in his seat, emphasizing what he was saying by pointing with his finger in the air. He was perspiring and hesitated just long enough to wipe his forehead. In his agitation he stood up and began to walk back and forth across the room.

"But do you know, for me as a boy the grandest insult was to our way of life. Do you know that our men worked as the servants of these district officers? Each of these women had three, four, five men and boys to do their every bidding, and it had to be done just so, just as these women wanted to have it, even if it was a way of eating and drinking we thought to be wrong. At the same time our women had to work in the fields and cut wood and make fires and clean the compounds. I would come back from the fields with my own mother and she would be tired and perspiring and she would have one of my little brothers or sisters tied to her back and there would be this woman with her house full of servants."

115

"I see you have servants as well," Stanley protested, still trying to blunt some of the Commissioner's anger.

"I have an official position here, and there are only the two of us. It isn't like one of the families here that has many hands to do the work. You didn't experience this, Morrison, so it is difficult for you to understand what I'm saying. Also you are a Christian, and you don't feel as Moslems do about alcohol. In the village where I grew up the people were entirely Moslems, but in the evening, every evening, if you walked by the District Officer's residence there on the verandah you would see his wife in fancy clothes taking a drink. I understand in the privacy of one's home one can have a certain leeway, but this was in the open, where the village children could see it, and they would come home and argue with their fathers because they could see the people there doing what they pleased. If the husband was off on a tour the wives did just the same every night. They put on their fancy clothes and they had the servants cook them a fancy dinner which they ate up by themselves. Then they sat out on the verandah holding their drinks.

"The women said they had work to do in the village, and they would come from compound to compound, but they didn't have a job to do. They only wanted to interfere. They wanted to tell our women how to prepare food, how to arrange the bedclothes, how to clean up the dishes. They tried to tell the women they should talk back to their husbands and not accept their husband's authority in family matters. They tried to tell women like my mother how to raise babies, and they didn't have babies themselves. Can you believe it, Morrison? They would tell us about babies when their husbands couldn't give them babies of their own. If they did have a baby they didn't try to raise it with us. When it was of a certain age they sent it off to England so it could have a proper education. The schools they talk so much about weren't even proper enough for their own children.

"And now they've left us, Morrison. But they've left us still

116

tied to their system with contracts and agreements and trade allotments and credit terms and there is still nothing in it for us. We could do it all for ourselves and we could move at more than this snail's pace we move in today. You see, Morrison, that is why I must swallow hard before I can have a man like that in my house."

13.

Mr. Smythe slept. He knew that he might suffer another heart attack, and he had brought all his medicines with him. He said nothing to Albert, but each of them understood what the other wasn't saying. He sat for a few moments talking with the old man who had come to see him; then his breathing became irregular again and he told the man to come back when he was better. He let Albert and his wife help him into his room and asked for a glass of water so he could take his pills. He slept through the night and on into the morning. He stirred from time to time. He dreamed.

He dreamed that he was walking. He was walking quickly without any sensation that his feet were touching the ground. He heard voices around him, but the faces he saw were motionless. People seemed to see him, but they paid no attention to him. There was the sound of voices and his feet moved over the dust. He had come into the village. Now he was walking down toward the river and the water rose to his feet and then he was drifting out on its reflection. He had fallen into the river, but he was somehow floating on its shining surface. The greenish gray current streamed past

118

him, then he was swimming in it with great strong strokes that pulled him effortlessly through the water. He turned onto his back, moving his shoulders into the furrows that marked the current's unending flow.

He dreamed. He heard voices talking, but again the people were not conscious of him. There were no faces, there were only the trees that hung over the water and he saw them from the water's glistening slickness and the trees swayed with wave-like movements as he passed under them. He was swimming again, his arms pulling him through the water as though his body had no weight. He found that when he rolled on his back he could see the sun and its glare was suffused through the film of the water that lapped over him. The sun's golden globe became a fiery halo through the water's reflecting lens and he closed his eyes. But as he closed his eyes he began swimming again, swimming blindly, and his arms carried him into a dimness that was cooler, that seemed to harden beneath him.

He found that he was swimming at the base of the pier, treading water silently in the gathering dusk. He pulled himself up the ladder on the side of the shaking wharf, but when he walked off the darkened boards he found that the ground had become a tended lawn, that there were lines of stones marking a path in front of him and it was still warm. It was sunset, but it was a different sunset. He had come to the garden of his cottage in England. He looked up at its windows, but there was no light showing so he started to move, but when he turned he had no idea of where he could go. He began milling his arms in circles, trying to find again the lightness, the strength he had felt in the water and he began slowly walking the boundaries of his garden.

He dreamed of flowers. The flowers that he plucked seemed always to be turned away from him when he lifted them to his face. They were wet with dew, but they were stiff and uncomfortable to touch. The stems were dry and unyielding. He dropped the handful he had picked and walked through the garden bending down to see the others.

119

The colors were different from what he remembered, somehow they'd changed. The roses, which he thought were white and yellow, were crimson and purple, and the leaves on the vines were thick and covered with a soft down. But when he touched a leaf it was shiny and hard. It was ivy, as he had known it would be. The flowers in his carefully tended English garden had become the flowers of his African garden, but the trees hanging over the edge of the wall were English trees, and as he stared up into them with his eyes shaded the light began to shift, to alter, the sky emptied and the dust brown ochre of the horizon that had given the dusk its soft lingering breathlessness became the stark distances of the African sky and the darkness came with the suddenness of Africa.

He dreamed of birds. At first of birds he couldn't see. He was walking in a part of the garden that was walled off from the trees where he could hear the birds stirring. The wall, as he walked further, became a fence held up with sagging sticks, and movements of the birds were visible as abrupt flutterings in the hanging clumps of bushes just beyond the fence. Then the sudden, darting bodies of the birds were visible as long feathered birds of paradise, crested in green and iridescent blue. One bird clung to a swaying branch not far from him, aware that he was looking at it, but letting itself be stared at. He had seen it somewhere before, perhaps in a book of exotic birds he had kept from his school days. The bird was all white except for a yellow curved beak, like a parrot's, and a cockatoo's crest which was a deep scarlet. He stood without moving, even though the bird had certainly seen him. It kept moving nervously on its wavering branch, turning its head from side to side to watch him. He bent down, trying to see its tail feathers, trying to see if it had the long curving tail feathers he remembered from the picture in his book, but he couldn't see through the dusty leaves.

He decided he wanted to tell someone about it and he slowly backed away, trying not to disturb the bird, but it fluttered from its branch and settled again on another

120

branch closer to him. He stood without breathing, pressing his hand against his chest and feeling his heart's irregular beating. The bird still swayed on its new perch, its head half turned away from him. He still had to tell someone about it and he turned to go back through the garden. But the garden had become larger than he remembered, and he seemed to be coming to a stretch of woods instead of the house. He walked into the shade of the trees and he felt his feet moving without touching the ground again and suddenly he was beside a river.

The waters where he had begun. The river he had grown up with when he was a boy. Curious to see if he could swim in it as he had swum in the African river he walked slowly down the soft bank, stepping carefully over the wild flowers. Small pale-blue petaled promises of violets, faded remembrances of forget-me-nots. He leaned clumsily over the water, stretching his arms in front of him, extending them over his lowered head as a child does for its uncertain first dive. He saw his face in the drifting current beneath him and it was his face as a boy. As he tried to think what this could mean he fell into the water with a splash that he didn't feel, only saw as the water spilled away from him. He found himself swimming with the same powerful strokes. He began to reach out with his arms, exulting in the strength he felt in his body. He saw the end of the woods at a distance beyond the curve in the river and he began swimming toward it, for moments pulling himself beneath the current and then twisting upward as he surfaced to look up through the fragmented beams of sunlight as they came down through the haze of leaves and shadow of the forest above him. At the edge of the forest he could see a hillside that was part of an English farm. He had been there when he was a child. He let himself float with the current, looking at the yellow-gold field. There was no one in the field. He could see no one in the cottage at the top of the hill. Behind the windows were drawn white curtains.

He dreamed. He saw a pier at the bottom of the golden

hillside. He began swimming again to look at it more closely. But the pier, as he came nearer to it, was the pier on the African river where he had first come to his station. It was the old pier, the one they'd replaced a year after he'd come. He stopped swimming again and let himself drift. He could see the pier from the African river leading to the path at the bottom of the English hillside and he suddenly became confused. He didn't know which of them he was coming back to. He didn't know which one he wanted to come back to.

He turned on his back again and the sun blinded his eyes. The glare dazzled him and he turned his head from side to side, feeling the water beneath him yielding to his weight like a pillow. The glare still blinded his eyes, the yellow, flashing, glaring light that flooded over him. He turned over on his stomach and began swimming again but the strength had gone out of his arms. His eyes tightly closed he felt himself being carried away by the current.

14.

He slept into the next day, but he slept fitfully. For moments he woke into the tangle of sounds that wove itself into the shadows of his room. He lay without moving, trying to place directions, trace patterns in the random noises; then he slept again. He couldn't have said precisely when he was asleep and when he was awake. The two states flowed into each other and there was no moment when he could tell that the one had begun and the other ended. He thought of himself as passively floating on the current of the river that he vaguely remembered from his dream. Even in the daytime his room was in shadow and once he woke, lying on his back. He found himself looking upward toward the ceiling, looking for the small reflection of the river's surface that he had always seen on the ceiling of his cabin on the ship. But there were only the muffled shadows that hung above him like darkening clouds. He was staring up into the acrid, clinging folds of the mosquito net.

He dreamed. He was lying on the bank of the river in the shadow of a bush. He found the air growing colder and he tried to move back into the sun. He couldn't raise his arms.

They were too heavy for him to lift. He lifted one knee but his body was so heavy he couldn't lift the other. With a groan he turned on his stomach, and his face, pressed against the sweaty pillow, seemed to be tasting the earth.

Sounds of children woke him. He woke to shouting on the other side of the compound fence as men struggled to untangle a donkey that had pulled its tether loose and wound it around a fence post. Birds woke him, their chirping at first filling his dream with bright flutterings of sunlight. The light seemed to be playing over the leaves of a bush outside his window. Outside the window of his office as he sat working. The swaying leaves of the palms in the garden outside his office door – letting the sun slip through onto the green bushes. The intermittent flashes glistened on the leaves. The glistening became the chirp of birds, the sound borne on the light wind. He opened his eyes, half expecting to see the bushes and the sunlight, but he was staring into the darkened corner of his room and the birds were outside on a bush, filling the air with their sounds. He slept.

He woke again, but not sure yet that he had wakened. Something he had heard in his sleep. Or had he heard it? A faint sound of whispering. Was it there? Yes. He heard it again. He tried to make out the words, but he could only hear the undertone of voices. Thinking someone had come to wake him he struggled to a sitting position. Opening his eyes he saw that the room was empty. From the deepened tone of the shadows he decided it must be afternoon. He leaned on an elbow, breathing heavily, uncertain as to whether he would sleep, waiting to sleep again. He fumbled with the clinging sheet, trying to smooth some of its creases. Did he hear it? Had the whispering begun again? He lay with his hand suspended over the sheet. Voices, somewhere behind him. With a nervous movement he turned his head. Was there someone in the room he couldn't see?

Behind the bed was a curtain. He leaned toward it and

124

heard the whispering again. Then he remembered that on the other side of the curtain was a window opening into the room in the back of the house, the room that Mr. Morrison rented. Without thinking he pulled back a corner of the curtain and found he could see into the room. The room, like his, was dim and shadowed, but his eyes were used to the darkness and he could make out figures in the shadows. On the bed on the other side of the room Mr. Morrison and the Commissioner's wife were embracing.

Involuntarily Mr. Smythe drew his head back, but his hand still held the curtain. For a moment he wasn't sure if he was still asleep. If this were part of another dream. He hesitated, then leaned down to look into the room again. It didn't seem to be something out of a dream. They were still wearing some of their clothes. He could see the loose white shape of Stanley's shirt. She had undone the buttons and her hands were inside it, her mouth against his chest. She was still whispering, but the sibilant hiss of her voice was muffled against the skin of his shoulders and neck. Her own blouse was hung carefully over the chair at the foot of the bed, her bra laid across it. Her slip had fallen to her waist and Mr. Smythe found himself staring at the dark outline of her small sharp breasts against the pale shape of the wall behind their bodies. He let the curtain fall and leaned back against the bed, closing his eyes, his breathing heavy and uneven again.

They shouldn't be doing that. For a moment his old habits as the authority for the district came back to him. That kind of thing couldn't be tolerated. But he had never seen a couple together. He found that he was almost overwhelmed with embarrassment. He wasn't as embarrassed for them as he was for himself. What would they think if they knew he had looked into the room? What would someone else think if they knew that he was lying close to the couple in the bed, that he could hear the sounds they were making. He strained to hear other noises in the house, opening of doors, footsteps, voices raised. It was quite still in the house. Albert and Nindi must be out, in the village somewhere. He was flooded with his own confusions. He pressed himself back against the pillow, trying not to hear the noises from the other room. He should say something. But what should he say? To whom should he say it?

There was a scratching of chickens close to the house, a child began crying, a cow tied to a fence in one of the compounds began bellowing uncomfortably. Agitated, feeling himself become more and more upset, he started to get out of the bed, but he still wasn't strong enough to walk, and he lay back again with his hand pressed to his heart. After a moment he found himself turning back toward the window. Without thinking, as if he were a child again, doing something that he was aware he shouldn't, he held his breath, leaned down, lifted the curtain and looked in at the man and woman in the other room. They were still whispering, but their mouths were against each other and the sound was only an incoherent sighing. She was lying beneath him, holding his body clasped against hers. They had pulled a sheet over them but as her legs lifted it dropped from them onto the floor. They tried to still the sounds of the creaking bed, but its yielding springs were too old to hold them silently. Her head began to twist back and forth on the pillow, her arms pulling his face down against her heaving chest.

Tony let the curtain drop. Shouldn't be doing that, either of them. He shouldn't be looking at them. Something a schoolboy would do. He listened for sounds in the house again. Nothing he should feel guilty about. It was the two of them who should be feeling something. Not him for discovering them. But he couldn't keep up his old feelings of moral consternation. When cases like this had come before him he had only heard the words, he had never had any idea of what the words could have meant. He had never known any of the people involved. It had never become personal, as this in the room beside him was personal. Somehow what was happening between them didn't fit into any of the categories that he had administered so sternly. In

126

the turmoil of his emotions he felt himself excusing them. He even felt an odd kind of tenderness toward them. As if they had let him experience something with them. It was something he thought he had lost in his life. He found himself listening to sounds again, for footsteps, doors opening, but now he was listening for them – to tell them if there were trouble. In some way he had become an accomplice in the simple reality of their embrace.

The whispering, the tumbling of the old bed ceased. There were sounds of movement, shoes cautiously scuffing on the concrete of the floor. Then he could hear a low murmur of talking. He was against the pillow again, his head turned toward the door. He saw himself as a kind of sentinel for them. When he felt himself sliding toward sleep again he dragged himself awake, opening his eyes, lifting his head so he could hear any disturbance in the house. He heard a sound of feet crossing the floor behind him; then the door into the back of the other room cautiously opened and slid shut. She had left. Still shouldn't be doing that. Only mean trouble. Had he spoken aloud? He dragged himself from his half sleep again. The house was breathing softly to itself. He hadn't spoken. He noticed it was darker in his room. It was close to the end of the afternoon. Sounds of the village preparing for the evening meal. Women calling. The steady thump of the mortars, the steady monotonous thump, like casual, uninspired drumming, like the fall of twigs on the metal roof. He slept.

He dreamed. He had come into the garden again, the garden he had dreamed of before. The same white bird was close to him again. It was on a branch beside him. He stopped walking and nervously reached his hand out toward it. It shied from him, sliding sideways. The leaves around it, green and hanging, hid it for a moment. Then it came toward him again, moving one foot at a time, its head dipping and bowing, the scarlet crest blurting out its stain of

127

color to him. He reached out to it again, holding his arm stiffly, not moving. Softly, carefully, it hopped onto his hand. He stared into its eyes. The yellow beak was closed and still. He began to raise the bird's white feathered body to his face and its wings lifted nervously, half raised in flight. Suddenly the bird flew at him and the wings flailed at his face and eyes, their white shape enveloping him, covering him in their wild flapping. But they beat without strength. Their whiteness was only a faint caress against his cheek.

He dreamed he was lying motionless but he could feel movement around him. He was on the ship and the current heaved below it. He was lying on the narrow bed in the cabin, but he wasn't alone. He could hear breathing, his hand pressed against a body in the bed beside him. His hand touched a naked thigh. It was his wife beside him, reaching toward him. Blindly he bent over her, straining to kiss her. His hand began to stroke her bare body. Then he was over-whelmed with embarrassment. He forced himself awake and lay staring into the darkness of the room. Couldn't let himself think about things like that. His wife. His wife. How well they had known this together.

He had thought, after her death, that he had lost this physical memory of their bodies together, but now it had come flooding back. For two people who know each other's bodies so well the memories become diffuse. They lose the consciousness of a single caress, a single embrace. He had spent one night with another woman, before he and Beverly were married, and he remembered that woman's body in a clearer way than he remembered his wife's, whom he had held and embraced so often. But what he was feeling now didn't seem to him to be a memory. It was a dream. He had loved her so much this way. It seemed to him now that this had been the most important part of their love for each other. This moment of forgetfullness, forgetfullness of everything except themselves. He had kept everything else at a distance by having her body there in his arms.

He lay in the dimness of the room remembering them

128

together. In the first years they were in the village, playing their stiff roles, it was as if they had a secret between them. He would catch her eye, he would turn and find her looking at him. And they would wait until the other dimensions of their life slowly peeled away. The petitioners would leave him alone, the people conferring to the last minute would rise to go, the servants who stood inside the door waiting for them to finish eating would slowly drift away to their own quarters. Then they would sit quietly for an hour, for form's sake. They didn't want anyone to find them in bed before it was the proper hour to sleep. Then they would turn to each other and with a suppressed trembling of excitement and laughter they would stand up, turn off the lights, and then hurry to their bedroom, already touching each other as they walked down the hallway. He was conscious that sometimes they giggled, the servants heard them, but at that moment neither of them cared.

He drifted again on the uncertain tides between sleeping and waking. He was touching his wife's body, but it twisted away as he touched it, its outline tangled in sheets and clothing. It was only the press of her mouth that kept him close to her, then her hand clenching over his. His hand was reaching down into the current of the river, he lifted it and let the water stream down his arm. It was water from their primitive wash stand as he sponged himself off before he came to the bed.

It wasn't only a physical hunger that had drawn them so close to each other. They were hungry for something else, for a moment when they could be alone. It was this they needed so fiercely, and it was this they gave each other, along with the movements of love, the tense fondling and the final embraces. They needed to feel that there was some place they could draw back to, where they could begin. From here they could take first steps, last steps.

The memory had almost lost itself. Perhaps he had hidden it away , since it was of so little use to him now. He was startled to find that it was still within him. The hands reaching toward each others' bodies in the murmuring room next to his had reached into him and found again the place where his memory of his body's love for her had lain hidden.

15.

"Jabi, isn't there any way you can keep him home?"

"You know there isn't. He'd think I was trying to get in the way of what he's doing. He was just the same when we first knew him."

"But then he was a young foolish person. Now he's a foolish person the same age we are."

Mr. Suso had come to Mr. Jabi's compound late in the morning, while Mr. Smythe was still drifting – half awake, half asleep – in his darkened bedroom. Albert had spent the first part of the morning trying to work, but he hadn't been able to begin. He forced himself to sit at his desk, but instead of writing the address he was supposed to deliver he looked at the wall beside the desk, or across the room at the window. Mr. Suso's footsteps on the stairs were an excuse for him to break off the morning's futility.

"Do you know, Suso, I think if I suggested too firmly that he stay indoors he would think I was trying to stop him from looking around in the village." They had moved onto the porch and they were sitting in the shade talking with their voices lowered, in case Mr. Smythe should wake up.

"What do you think he's trying to do?" Suso almost sighed as he spoke.

"I don't know. Something about the job."

"You don't think he could still be working in some way or another? We don't know everything that goes on down there at the coast. He could have been sent."

"No." Mr. Jabi shook his head. "I am sure that whatever he's doing it's something he's taken on himself. Do you think he is foolish, Suso?"

Suso shifted in his chair, sitting a moment with his lower lip pursed. "I don't like to use a word like that about someone who is so close a friend to you. Foolish isn't right. I don't know what to call him."

"Because he goes on with what he's doing?"

"How would it look, I ask you, Jabi, if I were to poke around now because for all those years I was considered to be the chief of the village? I think it would look – foolish, is the word I'd use."

"I would probably use the word 'sad', since Tony and I have known each other for so long. Certainly you wouldn't go looking around again since what you were doing then was just a job. Tony obviously finds that what he was doing was more than a job."

Suso stared off across the compound yard, squinting his eyes against the glare of the morning sun. "I don't know if I want anyone to think of himself as doing more than a job. That always seems to me to present difficulties for all the rest of us."

"But don't you have some of the same feelings? About what you did?"

"No. But it could be only because of the circumstances of how I came to the job. You, Jabi, felt somewhat like Tony."

Jabi shrugged self-consciously. "I think it is something teachers must fight against."

"Not in your case. I think you can be justified in thinking what you did was something more than just hours put in for pay."

132

"But Tony – it's the same thing."

"I don't know. I don't think it is the same. I think something else is also happening with him. It happens with men like him. If they go on, it begins to look as if they go on to prove that what they have been doing – needed to be done. I don't put it very well, Jabi. But you can follow what I am trying to say."

"I didn't realize you had given thought to this," Mr. Jabi said after a moment. Sitting back in his chair he seemed smaller and older, grayer than Suso as he stared out into the sunlight. When Suso didn't say anything, only sat and fanned himself, Jabi finally shrugged and went on. "There could be something in this, Suso. It is always difficult to draw a line – even for you and me, and if something has been left behind us, as Tony's work here was left behind him, then it begins to take on a different character. I think that what Tony looks back on as his job here isn't quite as the job really was."

"Do you think you could tell him that? Before the situation becomes difficult."

Mr. Jabi looked down at the floor of the porch, then he glanced at Suso and smiled. "That is very much the kind of opinion our new Commissioner would want to convey to me – so that I might pass it on to Tony. Don't tell me you're doing some of your old job, just as Tony is?"

Suso began to laugh. "It does sound like that, doesn't it? It reminds me of all those times I had to present messages to the Commissioner and the drift of the message came somehow at the tail end of all the little paragraphs that made up the beginning. Oh, Jabi – do you think we can ever learn to stop being ourselves?"

The sounds of the morning finally woke Mr. Smythe, but despite his new familiarity with them he lay in the bed looking around him, letting his eyes adjust to the pale streaks of shadow on the dim walls. He was confused by his dreams, and he was filled with conflicting emotions over what he'd seen in the other room. He put his feet over the edge of the bed and slowly forced himself to get up. He felt weak but there was no immediate protest from his heart. He couldn't stand another day in bed. The room smelled of his perspiration and insecticide and the mildewed mosquito net. He pulled on his shorts and knee socks, buttoned his shirt, and went into the front room. Mr. Jabi was alone again, sitting back at his desk with a piece of paper in front of him. He was toying with a pen, but the paper was blank. He looked up, surprised to see Tony on his feet, and frightened at how pale and drawn he looked.

"You shouldn't be up," he protested.

Tony sat down heavily in one of the chairs around the table. "Couldn't take another day in bed. A chap wastes away lying down like that. Have to be up and about or I forget how to put one foot in front of the other."

"Tony, you're not going out."

"No. Don't think I'm quite up to that. But I have things to do. Some impressions to get down on paper. You're doing the same."

Albert Jabi held up his hands. "It is to be a speech for a conference, but I have been thinking more of you. Are you well?"

"Albert, Albert," Tony was looking down at the toes of his shoes, "You mustn't fuss over me. Don't know if 'well' is the word to use. But I'll get by. No danger of anything happening to me while I still have things that must be done."

"Do you really think you should have made this long journey?"

"Of course. The journeying was the easiest part of it. It's coming back to so much that's unfinished that's hard. The heat as well. I always forget how hard it was when I went on leave. You remember. Sometimes I'd near faint dead away when you'd all line up to give me the welcome back on post. Standing there in my sun helmet and all of you swimming in front of my eyes."

134

"You didn't show it."

"Comes with the responsibility. Do you think I could skip over the eggs today? Something more in the African style would suit me, I think."

Albert stood up and went hurriedly toward the kitchen. "I don't know if Nindi has heard you. Of course have our breakfast. But you must begin with tea. You absolutely must begin with tea. It will give you strength."

He found that he couldn't finish the bowl that Nindi brought him, the boiled millet, curdled milk and honey, but it tasted so good to him. She protested that he must have eggs as well, but he thanked her for letting him have what he'd asked for. She kept fussing over him, like her husband disturbed at Tony's pallor.

"You must rest," she said finally, looking down at him with a worried expression.

"I have nothing to do but rest. You mustn't carry on over me. I'm going to sit here and write a bit. Nothing more tiring than that."

"I can go for anything you need." She was standing on the other side of the table, dressed in her usual loose robe and turban wrapped around her head. She was holding her hands in front of her and for a moment Tony was reminded of his own mother's gestures. He had to close his eyes for a moment, and when he opened them she had anxiously come around the table toward him. He could see from her face that he had frightened her.

"Good to smell the old smells again," he said hurriedly as an explanation. "All of it mixed together. It takes me back." He sat without moving, smiling up at her until she abruptly took his bowl and went toward the kitchen. She stopped at the door, trying not to look as upset as she felt. "You must say if there's anything to be done. Beverly would want us to take care of you, you know that."

He nodded carefully. "Yes, I know it."

He left the room, but he came back with a notebook and a folder of papers. Albert, who was sitting at his desk again, asked him if he had reports to do. Tony spread his papers out on the table and looked at him sharply. After a moment he nodded. "Just want to get some impressions down. Could say it's a report to myself."

The two men worked for the rest of the day, occasionally calling out something for the other to laugh over. Nindi brought them meat and rice at midday. They sat talking for an hour, Nindi sitting in the room with them, though she was in a chair against the wall; then they went back to their papers. When school finished there was the noise again of the children leaving. A few moments later came the sound of people calling out to the teacher. Mr. Morrison came in through the back of the compound and went into his room through his own door. Tony sat uncomfortably listening for footsteps, but the room was far enough from the center of the house for sounds to be distant and muffled. They would blend in with the noises of the afternoon if someone weren't listening hard. He was looking at his notes again when there was a sound behind him and he looked around. Stanley had come into the room without his shoes, trying to be as quiet as possible. Tony was embarrassed. He didn't want the other man to know that he hadn't been sleeping the day before. Stanley saw him at the table and smiled broadly.

"So you're up!"

"After all that sleep I thought I'd try to do a little work. Can't just lie around."

"You slept all day yesterday?" Stanley was asking in a casual tone, but Tony thought he sensed an undertone behind the easy manner.

"Slept like a log the entire time. Didn't know anything until this morning," he said emphatically, at the same time moving papers around in front of him to mask his embarrassment.

"All that sleep seems to have picked you up again," Stanley said, still smiling.

136

"But he's promised not to do anything," Albert called in from his study.

"I won't tax him," Stanley answered. "I was only coming in to see how he was making it today."

"Thanks," Tony responded. "On the mend, you can say. Just taking it easy will do the trick." He finally made himself look at Mr. Morrison, but he found he couldn't relate the concerned, smiling young school teacher standing across the room from him with the figure he'd seen in the semi-darkness the day before. But at the same time he knew they were both the same person. He wondered if he had seemed like this as well – that he had more than one face, more than one physical person, but that someone who knew him saw only one, and had no idea of the others. He nodded to Stanley uncomfortably. "Have to get back to these notes." Stanley gestured to make it clear he understood and went back along the hallway to his room, making as little noise when he left as he had when he'd come.

"Nice of him to come in," Tony said noncommitally.

"He is quite a nice person," Albert agreed from the other room.

"Wouldn't be surprised if other people think so as well."

"No," Albert said carefully, "I wouldn't be surprised at it myself."

After they'd eaten supper, despite their protests, he insisted on leaving the house.

"I can't just stay in, and you two have put up with me for two days now. I only want to call on some of the chaps from the old days."

"I can walk with you," Albert insisted.

"It's dark now and there's only a touch of heat left. The doctor himself told me that if I felt like a bit of exercise it would be the best thing for me." He was already standing at the door with his papers under his arm.

"Tony," Albert began, then stopped, realizing it was

137

useless to continue. "If you're tired send word and I'll come and walk back with you."

Tony hesitated at the door, for a moment looking tired and uncertain. "I will, of course. But can't think of that happening. Things I have to get on with, lots of old friends I have to say hello to. All the chaps who came to see me the first night. Never forget that. I do think it's only right to drop by, give them my regards in a little more personal setting. Always seemed to be the best way."

"But you must send word if you want a companion on the walk home," Albert called after him as Tony went out the door and slowly crossed the darkened porch to the stairs. "You've got me started on some of your old habits again. I'll be here working until you get back."

16.

In the morning he went out again, despite their protests.

"I'll be back in before the heat is at its worst, and by this time I'm getting a bit used to it," he said firmly. He settled his stained sunhelmet on his head and took his papers under his arm.

"I could go with you," Albert remonstrated.

"Just one of my inspection walks. Nothing anyone else need bother with, and I know you have your speech to do."

They could see the uneven shape of the sun helmet over the top of the fence as he made his way along the path into the village. When it grew hotter he was back, perspiring a little, the papers under his arm wilting from the humidity.

"What did you find?" Albert asked from his study when Tony dropped his hat on the table in the other room and sat down, wiping his face with a handkerchief.

"Things haven't changed much. Not in any way I would have expected. Same channels of trade, same system for getting stuffs to the market. Still even some of the same people doing the job just the way they've always done it."

"What did you expect?" Albert's interest was genuine. He

put down his pen and came into the other room to sit with Tony.

"I had the impression when I turned over my office that there were a number of schemes to get things going here. New ways to get crops into the ground. Better organization to sell all the surplus." Again, the dry, ironic tone had come into his voice.

"In some ways there has been a step forward," Albert said defensively. "You know what the problems are. They are just the same as they were then. The soil is poor, there isn't enough rain, our methods of agriculture are too unsophisticated. That hasn't changed." He stopped and shook his head. "In one way it was easier for everyone when you were here. They could say that you were to be blamed for our backwardness and our poverty. Now it seems they can blame you for trade agreements and poor prices for what we do manage to export, but the truth of the matter is that we can grow very little for export. It was easier not to look back to our old past, even if we remembered that the history we knew from the singers said over and over again that the life here was always poor and people were hungry. They quarrelled over food, they fought each other over water, they took each other as slaves to do their work.

"And then for a time you were here. I know from your tone that you have thought much about it. I think of it as well, you know? The colonial administration here lasted sixty years – that's all – but I think at first the people expected you would change everything. That the rain would fall, that the grass would grow, and within a generation or two the land would be something besides the burnt-over half desert that it has always been."

"But we disappointed them," Tony laughed ironically.

"Yes." Albert was still serious. "You did, so it was only natural for everyone to blame you. You must have been disappointed yourself."

"The pace was slower than I'd hoped. I didn't think it would take so long to get some kind of order here. Were you

140

disappointed? You worked alongside me."

"A little."

"And you thought it might be better when I was gone."

"I didn't think miracles would take place – but there were so many speeches – you know you always want to be optimistic."

"So you didn't believe in all this colonial romance." Tony's voice had become tight again, and he was looking away from Albert.

Albert began laughing, and Tony looked at him with surprise.

"Do you know, all we saw of the Empire – even when we were part of it – was a man at a table who was much too hot and a flag that drooped behind on a tree trunk that someone had peeled the bark from. All the rest of it we had to take your word for."

Tony laughed with him and after a moment shook his head. "Then I must not have been very convincing."

"You were, Tony, you were. You were here at least, and we could see what it was you were trying to do. Most of the time that was enough."

"I dare say you don't include this kind of talk in the speeches you give today."

"But Tony, remember, speeches must always be optimistic. Yours always were. But I don't have as much to do and I think too much about all of it." Albert shrugged. "There is something you must grant us. The number of cattle has greatly increased." His tone was lightly mocking, like Tony's.

"Yes, I see signs of it. You and I did so much to keep the numbers down. Tried to introduce better stock. But it's the same old thing. Everyone wants to have as many as possible. Get a step ahead of the fellow in the next compound. I don't see a blade of grass left out there."

"One compensation, there is a market for our cattle just now. More than it was before. I believe the price is fairly high."

141

Tony looked at him a moment before he answered. He put his hand on the bundle of papers he'd dropped on the table. "Yes, the price is not bad, considering the quality of the cattle they're bringing in. Most of them worth more for their hide and bones than for any meat that's on them."

"And if you come away from this village and think of what is occurring in other areas you must say that we have made some steps forward. It is only that we are still much poorer than we thought we would be."

"As you say," Tony conceded, his irritation past. "I couldn't make it rain. The one thing they forget to teach us when we were doing our course."

He went out again later in the day, his sun helmet firmly pulled down on his head and his papers under his arms. He spent considerable time with the old men he'd known from his time there. They laughed and told stories about each other, and he asked them things from time to time and sometimes he wrote something down on his papers. He couldn't talk as easily with the younger men. They were uncomfortable with him; since they had so little idea of what he'd been doing there. Many of them had come into the village from isolated compounds in the bush and they couldn't talk with him at all. He bore down on them with his shorts flapping and his mustache working and they tried to get out of his way. He still spoke the languages of the area, but he had been away for ten years and some of his expressions weren't in use any more. If he did manage to get some of the young men into a situation where they couldn't avoid talking he often surprised them with questions about the crops and the cattle that were difficult to answer easily. And sometimes he would write something down on his papers.

When he came back to the house it was long after it was dark and he was too tired to sit up. He talked for a moment about some of the old men he had seen, then said he was going to get some sleep. Had to watch himself until he was

142

completely mended. The next morning, again over protests, he went out as soon as they'd eaten breakfast. This time he had a tape measure with him, and people in the village saw him sliding down earth banks to measure sewer pipes or concrete abutments. He bent over the bridges that had been constructed at the edge of the village to check their underpinnings. For nearly an hour he was busy at the wharf looking at the pilings and going through the materials that were stored in the shed. If someone came to talk to him he immediately began asking questions, papers and pen ready to write down answers. Most people left him alone.

In the afternoon, when it was cooler, he left again, saying only to Jabi that he wanted to see some of the cultivation at first hand. He went along the main street past the open shops, nodding to the shopkeepers that he knew. When he got to the edge of the village he realized that it was still hot, hotter than he had expected, but he was too impatient to wait for the sun to drop lower. He walked past the last thatched huts, following the trampled path of the cattle and goats. There were marks of truck tires but he didn't know when they'd been made. In the soft dust they could have been made an hour before or a week before. He thought perhaps they led to the new cultivated areas. As he walked he was conscious of how dry and sparse it was. It was a sparseness that the rains wouldn't alleviate. He remembered that the rains turned the earth green and that the spindly bushes put out lines of small, clenched leaves, but that the growth never became dense or thick. When he'd first come to Africa he'd expected to see the jungle he'd read about, instead there was this dry, tough growth. Except for the scattered trees it reminded him of the weeds that sprang up in the empty lots in the cities he'd grown up in.

He was walking east along the river, though he was a few hundred yards away from it and he couldn't see it through the bushes. The sun was behind him and he could feel its weight beginning to press down. When he'd gone a mile he felt the first low buzzing in his ears, and the light at the

143

horizon began to darken. He stopped, looking for shade. It had happened to him so often before that he was almost used to it. A kind of dizziness that came from too much sun, the beginnings of heat stroke. There were no trees close to him, only low bushes. Stiffly he bent and crawled into a thicket close to the path. It formed a kind of shade, enough to protect him. He sat on the hardened dirt and waited for the dizziness to pass. He felt himself beginning to hallucinate. The birds' whistles seemed to be coming through a heavy layer of dust and earth, the sky was hanging over him like a kind of sagging cap. He leaned back against the bushes, feeling the thorns pick at his shirt. He closed his eyes. Slowly the buzzing stopped, the noises became clearer. When he opened his eyes he could see the distant haze that marked the bleached blue of the sky where it met the earth. After a moment he stood up and began walking again.

In the next hour he had to stop two more times to fight off dizziness. No one knew where he was and if he did faint they wouldn't know where to look for him. Had to keep walking. Carelessness. He didn't used to be so careless. He was trying to follow the tire tracks but the path had divided and sub-divided so many times he wasn't sure what he was following. At several divisions of the path there were tire tracks leading in different directions. He finally came to a halt, standing under a scraggly tree, breathing heavily, looking around him. It looked the same everywhere he turned. The irregularly shaped trees with their listless foliage against the thin sky, the twisted bushes below them. He knew he was only two or three miles from the village, but he could have been anywhere in hundreds of miles of bush and it would have looked exactly the same. He had forgotten the intractability of the land. He had forgotten its hard emptiness. He felt a touch of fear, just as he'd done on his first walks years before. He turned around and began following his own foot-steps back through the thicket.

He was walking toward the sun now. It hung in front of him in a deep red-orange ball. Through the film of haze it

144

seemed to be breathing in short, shallow gasps. As he made his way through the bushes he realized that it was his own breathing he was hearing. Close to him there was a crashing sound. Cattle coming in to the village. They were walking slowly, a tall man with a long stick trailing after them, driving them in front of him with shouts and flicks of the stick. Tony felt easier. Even if the man hadn't turned to look at him he knew he was there. If Tony couldn't make it back they would know where to come for him. The ground now was stripped by the herds of cattle that had grazed back and forth over it. The earth was indented with the marks of hooves. The grass had been bitten so close, first by the cattle and then by the goats, that it was only a half-visible stubble on the surface of the ground. As he crossed a clearing he kicked away cattle droppings that the sun had turned into dull, hard pebbles. When he came in sight of the first meandering line of woven fences he felt some of the same relief that the first African travelers must have felt when they made their way through the bush, never sure what they were coming to – or if there was anything there – after they'd walked so far.

The next morning he was standing on the wharf looking down into the river when someone came toward him. It was one of the young men. He couldn't remember talking to him before.

"The Commissioner wonders where you are off to and he would like to see you if you have a moment." The man stood diffidently a few steps away from him. Tony was momentarily confused.

"Don't know where I'm off to myself."

"He would like you to drop by the office. He thought you would like to see it again." The man was very young and his English still sounded like a classroom exercise. Tony wiped his face, giving himself a moment to think. "Want to walk about a bit more. Tell him I'll drop in when the sun gets up a bit."

When he came to the Commissioner's office an hour later he had the same flood of emotions that he'd felt at the residence. He had also built the office and it had changed even less than the other building. Only the portraits on the walls had changed, he noticed wryly, the portraits and the window screens that gaped open where they had ripped and not been repaired. The Commissioner's desk was the same one he'd sat behind. There was a new chair. He hadn't noticed it until Mr. Camara motioned him toward it.

"You must sit. You haven't been well." The Commissioner had on another khaki bush shirt that looked vaguely like a uniform. He was so much darker skinned than most of the other people in the village that he seemed almost like a foreigner. Tony had always taken his own skin color for granted, forgetting sometimes that he did look so unlike the others, but he had always been conscious of the differences between the local tribal groups. Mr. Camara still seemed out of place to him.

"How are you feeling now?" Camara asked, trying again to be hearty, but at the same time watching the other man closely.

"Still not myself, but the doctor told me I should be up and about as soon as I feel up to it." His eyes were going around the room as he answered. Mr. Camara followed his glance.

"This must have memories for you as well."

"Yes, rather."

"It was indeed the center of your empire here."

Tony was silent. "Nothing's changed except the portrait on the wall," he said finally.

"I could understand that would seem a bit amiss to you."

Tony turned his head to look around him. Like the room in the residence the office was so familiar to him, but it had a different reality for him. At the same time it still had the old remembered reality and he couldn't yet find where they meshed. One was a half dream, the other was a half comprehended present. He still wasn't able to put the two together.

146

"What have you been finding in your inspection tours of the village?" Camara asked in an effort at lightness.

"Just visits to old friends. Finding my way about the old place again."

"You have asked so many questions."

"I've been away for some time. A chap likes to put himself in the picture."

"All the same, it reminds me of the official visits the local officers used to make in the district where I grew up."

Tony carefully crossed his legs and put his sun helmet on his knee. "Just an old campaigner going through his drill."

"Something so simple as that?"

"A chap doesn't like to think he's forgotten what he used to know."

"You have been taking considerable notes. I think you probably have found things which I would find of interest."

Tony shook his head. "Just filling in details. You might say it's a memorandum to myself."

"All the same I would find it interesting."

Tony could feel the pressure the other man was putting on him. He moved a little in his chair. "Perhaps, when I have it all in better order."

They watched each other over the desk. Finally Camara broke the silence. He lifted up a sheaf of crumpled, unevenly scrawled papers. "I'm sure this is another sight you remember well. All the petitions that find their way to us. Was it always so that we were expected to be able to solve the problems of the universe?"

Tony laughed shortly. "For a time I thought I could."

17.

He slept badly. He finally drifted into a light slumber an hour before dawn and was dragged back to wakefulness by the shrill crowing of the roosters. His eyes closed again, but he was wakened by the thump of the women pounding millet for breakfast. He stared up into the folds of the mosquito netting. He felt stifled by the musty smell, but at the same time it was a smell that was so familiar to him. Reluctantly he pulled himself up, pushed the curtains to one side and sat on the edge of the bed. He didn't feel as strong as he had the day before. It had to be the heat. He would stay out of it for the day. He had enough to do with the notes he'd taken already.

Albert had to leave after breakfast to sort through some materials that had come to the school, and when he returned to eat lunch Tony had moved onto the porch and his chair was surrounded with pieces of paper. His thin body was bent over them, his hands sorting through them and busily marking one or another with a pen.

"What have you here?" Albert asked.

"Something I've been working on. Interesting to see it all

laid out." He was still working with the papers as he spoke, his manner withdrawn and distracted.

"Come to dinner. I know it will soon be ready."

A moment later Tony followed him into the room. He wiped his forehead on his sleeve. He sat down at the table without looking up.

"I didn't see you go out this morning," Albert said after a moment.

"No need to go out for the present. Enough to do to keep me here."

Nindi brought in food, the inevitable cooked meat and rice, and they ate quickly. She sat in a corner, wrapping her robe closer to her, watching them.

"You are so quiet both of you," she said timidly.

"I don't want Tony to tire himself," Albert answered.

"No worries on that score," Tony said quickly. "I'm feeling fit again. Just things on my mind. Didn't mean to be a stick."

"I don't think of you as a stick." She was almost apologetic. "You are so much alike. When he wants to think something through," and she nodded to her husband," he sits like that. I've seen you both sit for hours without a word when there was something you couldn't decide."

"Perhaps we will sit that way today," Albert said to his wife.

"You have your work to do," Tony said. "I didn't know that you still were so taken up with duties." He had become interested again.

"It isn't anything so important."

Tony spread his hands out on the table. It was obvious he was struggling with his irritation again. The light had softened in the room, but there was a hard glare to the flaring patterns of sun that spread themselves just inside the door and windows. He seemed to be staring into the brightness, as if he could puzzle something out in its certain forms. He was trying to be silent, but his emotions were becoming too much for him to hold back. He pulled at his mustache and then sat back in the chair, crossing his arms over his chest.

149

"I didn't have a thing to do when I left here. You know that, of course. Not a thing. It's no good to do that to someone."

Mr. Jabi gave a deprecating shrug. "It could be that people want to listen to me speak because there were so few of us doing any jobs at that time. Could it be that there were too many of you?"

Tony burst into laughter, a short, self-derisive laughter. "I was so long out here by myself I never thought of myself as the many. Never in the course of history have so few owed so little to so many. But yes. Probably right. When you collected us all up there were a lot of us, and we'd all come back to Britain at once. The whole thing went down like someone had put a pin in a balloon. Rotten shame the Americans didn't decide to build up some sort of colony on the moon. Would have suited us all." He looked away, then drummed his long fingers on the table top. "But no use going over that old ground. Worn out its welcome I would say."

He stood up and fussed with his rolled-up sleeves. He was still wearing his old clothes, but they had picked up new wrinkles and now they seemed again to be part of his body. He went toward the door. "Nindi, thank you. Albert, if there's a minute I'd like you to look at one or two things here."

Albert followed him slowly, uncomfortable at Tony's sudden official air. Tony bent down and gathered up the papers; then he looked carefully around the compound yard from the porch. Though it was empty, and the path seemed to be deserted on the other side of the rusting metal fence, he appeared to be dissatisfied. "Don't like it here. Better to talk inside."

He led the way into Albert's study, spread out his papers and picked up the top sheets. He cleared his throat, though Albert was already listening. "I didn't feel I was finished with the job I was doing, and when I first had the little walk around with you I could see that the job we'd started here wasn't finished at all. But I'd had a sixth sense this was what I

150

was going to find and I was prepared for it."

Albert turned toward his desk, apprehensive of whatever it was Tony wanted to tell him. He remembered when Tony's manner was so official he was often difficult to reason with. Tony had drawn himself up, papers in hand. Did he have to go on with it, Albert wondered, realizing as he asked himself the question that this side was as much a part of Tony as the side that he knew from their friendship.

"As I said, Albert, I did expect to find something like this before I came up here. I don't have much weight now, but my name was still known to some of the old staff in the allocations section. I took down some figures from their books. Spent a few days going over the records. Shouldn't have had such a look-see, perhaps, but some of the chaps were most obliging." He stopped but Albert was silent, rolling one of his pencils on his desk.

"In the last two days I've been endeavoring to follow up on some of these figures and I have been told a different story by the people here. The funds that were to go to maintenance and repair have evaporated somewhere between the allocations office and the people who were to do the work."

Albert realized he would have to say something. As he fiddled with the pencil he tried to consider the possible answers he could make. He understood immediately that he couldn't side with Tony in any way and continue his own relationship with the Commissioner, or with any Commissioner who would come to replace him, and he wondered if any of it would make any difference, whatever Tony had in mind. "It has been difficult to get funds to do the necessary work for many of our projects," he said finally.

"It isn't a difficulty that I'm talking about. All the figures here make it clear that we have a case of theft."

"It has been some time since I visited the allocations office." Albert's voice was expressionless.

"I think it's been going on for some time. Don't know which of the new Commissioners started it, but it's still going

151

on. Part of Camara's job is to supervise the purchase of cattle to get meat for the tourist hotels. I've been talking with the herders, chaps he's buying from. He's paying them half what he's charging the government. The difference is staying in his own pocket.

"I went through all the specifications for pipes and drains and the lot. Maybe you don't expect the new chaps to know what they're dealing with, but in my day we had to know what materials were, whether they were up to the job. Everything I've looked at – the drains, the concrete work, the repairs to the road – everything's been substandard, but the costs given to the allocations office have been for top standard materials. I have it all here." He held out one of the papers to Mr. Jabi.

"The allocations officer used to be a man by the name of Edwards. But that was some time ago. I think there must be someone different there now." Mr. Jabi's voice stayed flat and dry. He had pushed the pencil away and he was leaning back in his chair, looking past Mr. Smythe toward the cobweb of lines on the map over his desk.

Tony went on confused. "But it's all here. On paper. It's theft I'm talking about. Not just your ordinary carelessness. Always be a little of that in the best run administration. It's just plain theft."

As he finished Albert felt that a kind of chasm had opened between them. It was the tone in his voice. Albert could hear his pleased excitement. Mr. Smythe had expected there would be corruption, and now he was happy that he had found it. He had hoped they would fail without him, and this was clear proof that they had. For a moment Albert wanted to argue, to protest, to tell him that despite their inexperience, their lack of money, despite the drift of the first years when they were working by themselves, they had managed to keep their new society going. But the dishonesty he saw as well as anyone didn't give him any pleasure, instead it left him dismayed and unhappy. That was the difference between them. And he couldn't see any

152

reason to say that either. Beyond some kind of vindication for his old friend he didn't feel that it would make any difference at all, and it suddenly became important for him to keep himself at a distance.

"From time to time there have been questions asked as to the resources we have at our disposal for rebuilding and maintenance. The questions have all been answered satisfactorily. I haven't thought any more about it." He was still looking away from the other man.

"If someone had been on his toes this could have been nipped when it first started."

"We often have questions of a similar sort in the education department. It is true that in the past there has been some mismanagement of funds, but this was brought to our attention by people from the allocations office. I think the most useful thing would be to wait for them to say something in this instance."

"Albert," Tony sat down across the room from him. They had often sat in the same chairs and argued in the past, but they both realized that the past had receded, and that they found themselves in an uncomfortable present. "You know how I ran the show here. Never a question of funds or how they were used. You were with me when we went over the papers and figures year after year. You can't let this go past. What kind of example does it set?"

Albert stared out of the window at the sun-baked yard. He realized that for the first time in the years that they had known each other he was impatient with Mr. Smythe. He turned away from the window and looked across into Tony's face. Tony was standing again with his papers, one hand brushing at his mustache.

"It was often very tiresome to have to spend so many hours working out the accounts for my school when there was never enough money, and what little money I got was simply handed over to me. I wasn't asked how much I thought I would need or how I thought the funds should be used." His voice was level, and he shrugged apologetically

153

when he'd spoken, but Tony drew back, surprised. He sensed that he had come close to something in the other man that he didn't fully understand.

"I think we all felt that way from time to time," he said finally.

"Those of you sent out to work in the colonies sometimes lived in rather primitive conditions, but the salaries were quite in excess of those people working under you. Your salaries I understand compared quite favorably with those paid to a worker in England itself. Those in lesser positions, the African clerks and so on, were much less favorably salaried. I think you would find in this some reason perhaps why there was much less temptation to use funds unwisely among the colonial officers themselves."

Tony had listened to the beginning of what Albert was trying to say, but by the end he was holding out his papers again, shaking them back and forth.

"No. It won't wash, Jabi . . . Albert. It isn't salaries that I'm talking about. I'm not talking about expediency or explanations or anything else. It's theft out and out. Clear cut. Everything I have down on paper here tells me one thing. I've seen too much of it not to know it when I see it. It's theft and embezzlement and misuse and carelessness – the whole lot at once. It isn't that you have to put up with this, you can't tell me that."

Mr. Jabi drew back from the indignation in Mr. Smythe's voice. He realized with some sadness that his cautious effort to have the other man think of the situation from another perspective only meant that he would have to defend the present Commissioner, and he could see immediately that he had put himself in a hopeless position. Smythe, as had happened so often before, was right. Clearly and unassailably right. Mr. Jabi bent his head.

"I'm not putting up with something, as you say. I am only saying that I see sides to the situation that I once didn't see. It doesn't seem to be as simple as it once did."

"My dear chap, I'd say that's the heart of it right there. It's

154

all down here on paper, and it's as simple as you could ask for."

Mr. Jabi started to answer, then he picked up his pencil again. "I am sometimes not as much in touch with things as I should be."

Tony straightened up, dropped his papers on the table and ran his fingers through his hair. He again assumed his official manner, but Albert could hear the triumphant tone that had come back into his voice.

"This is that one time when it is simple for once. Not like one of those mess-ups I used to have from time to time when none of the figures would come out right. This time there's no question. When I do my report I won't have to do anything more than point out the figures. Couldn't be anything simpler under the sun."

"Who will you prepare your report for?" Albert's tone was incredulous.

"There's a staff that takes care of this. Has to be. They'll know careful work when they see it. I did have a job to do here after all, Albert. Things still left to be finished. No one can say that I let my people down."

18.

Later in the day Tony came back into Albert's study.

"Some things I want to go into a little more deeply." He had his papers under his arm and he was holding his sun helmet.

"But should you go out?" Albert had been so busy with his own work that he had forgotten most of what they'd said earlier. "It's still very hot."

"You understand how important it is that I go on with it now. A few more questions and I'll have it sorted out. Could be one of the most important things I've done here."

He started toward the porch, squinting his eyes against the glare of the afternoon sun. "Can't tell a job just to wait until the sun goes down." He strode across the dusty yard and went through the compound gate.

An hour later Albert heard voices shouting outside his fence. People were calling questions, there were shouted answers. Two young men in grimy undershirts and tattered shorts came through the gate supporting Mr. Smythe between them. One was carrying a rumpled handful of papers, the other had the

156

old sun helmet. Albert called out to Nindi and he hurried down the steps toward them. Tony's head rolled against one of the men's shoulders. When they came to a stop his eyes opened.

"Good. Got me back," he said finally in an uneven whisper. "Not quite up to it yet."

The men explained that they had found him unconscious at the end of the old drainage system. He'd fallen down the bank and was lying in the dirt. Tony tried to lift his head, and still holding on to their arms, his thin body taller than theirs by several inches, he tried to take a step by himself. They kept their places beside him to keep him from falling. "Fainted again." He looked at Albert, his expression pleading. "Still not used to the sun. Just when I think I've got everything in hand it gets away from me."

The three of them half lifted him up the steps, Nindi following them with the helmet and the papers. The young men had been on their way from the grazing grounds to their own compounds and they were anxious to leave. Albert asked them a few more questions, as much as anything to give himself a little more time before he had to go back to the room and see his friend's drawn face. Finally he told them he and the old D.O. thanked them and they went quickly across the yard and out the gate.

In the darkness of the room Tony was lying back across the bed, his head propped up on a pillow. His breathing was hoarse and shallow, but his eyes were open.

"Bit of a fright there. Never know where you're going to light when you faint away like that."

"You must have tablets for this. You should take medicine now." Albert's voice was muffled as he tried to cover his anxiety, his small body bending as he leaned down over the bed. The mosquito net was hanging in low folds just above them and he pushed it back impatiently, afraid of its stifling smells.

Tony started to sit up, then lay against his pillow again. "In my bag at the foot of the bed. Be better in a minute, but there's no use taking a chance. I'll take my medicine." His voice was a little stronger, but he was still half whispering. He was pulling at

157

the front of his shirt with his hand. He had perspired as he lay on the ground and the shirt was dark and wet. Nindi hurried to the kitchen and came back with a glass of water. They stood watching him as he swallowed capsules from two of his bottles. He coughed to clear his throat, then looked up sharply. "I had the papers with me."

"I believe everything is here," Albert said. "The men brought everything they found with you."

"Then I'd best get a spot of rest. Damned sorry about this. You two shouldn't have to put up with this nonsense."

They both stayed in the room with him. It wasn't until his eyes slowly closed and his breathing became deep and even that they left him alone.

Later, when it had grown dark and the noises of the village had dwindled to a music program from the government radio station and the voices of children calling to each other along the pathways, Albert came back into the room. He had brought food, but he was uncertain about leaving it. He had brought a lantern with him and its yellow flame cast dim shadows over the figure on the bed. As he stood undecided, the bowl of food in one hand and the lantern in the other, Tony lifted his arm.

"If that's supper I won't pass it by." His voice was weak, but he was trying to sound cheerful. "If I could have tea as well. Don't mean to be a bother, but it would help me get my strength back."

"Nindi has already cooked it. I'll bring it when you've had something to eat."

When he'd emptied the bowl Tony lay back against the pillow. "Sit, if you have a minute."

"It is early," Albert said. "I will come back with the tea and a chair." He went into the other room and came back with Tony's cup.

"A chap feels a bit awkward when he pulls something like this. Falling down on your bloody doorstep."

"But how many times did we nurse each other in the old

158

days? When you're out in a place like this you have to watch out for each other. You came to us so many times with medicines," Albert protested.

"We did do that, didn't we? But I didn't think I was still so far from fit. Just shows that you don't know yourself as well as you think. Too much sun. Does it every time."

"You have also done too much. I mean in a physical way," Albert added hurriedly. "You have been out in the heat too much."

"I saw so much that needed checking into. Wanted to do it all at once." He was silent for a moment. "I forgot sometimes that so much time had gone past. I carried on just like I was still on the job. I have my report to do, but no hurry with it. Let it take its time. It's waited long enough. I'm sorry too . . . don't know how to say it. Sorry that I didn't give you some sign as to what I was up to. Must have seemed a bit odd, all that running about."

"It was much like the old days. I often didn't know what you had in your head to do then."

"I didn't think of anything then. Just the job to be done." He suddenly laughed, his voice still weak, but with some of his insistence coming back. "I say that now, but it wasn't like that. I often didn't know what I was going to do next and I used to come to you to talk it out. We talked a great deal about how we were going to get on with it."

"You often talked a great deal about it. I was still so new to all of it that I couldn't imagine any other way of doing things. So I listened to you."

"I had some glimmering today." Tony began awkwardly, "that you had ideas of your own about how I was going about things. Must have happened more than once when I was holding forth in the old days."

"We come from such different backgrounds. I don't think I knew myself how different it was for us until after it was all over and you'd gone. I couldn't have told you then that despite our friendship I was certainly intimidated by you."

Albert stared into the lantern's flickering yellow eye of light as he went on. "There was so much that wasn't

159

intended. Do you know it was easier for those others, that fellow you had set up as the chief, Suso – or the Alhaji. They had no idea of where you'd come from or what you were doing. Often you were more of an annoyance to them than anything else. When they wanted you for a petition or to settle a case in court they still didn't know all the background you brought to bear on it. But people like me, we had just enough schooling so we could accept the position you had given yourself. We could understand it the way the others couldn't. We even felt ourselves to be part of the system. We'd had enough education to think of ourselves working with you, but we knew we were down at the bottom. There was a ladder to success, but I don't think we felt we succeeded to come to the bottommost rung. Suso didn't think himself part of your system at all; so he never thought of himself at the bottom of anything. But I couldn't help being intimidated by you."

"That's a rather grim picture you paint of it all." Tony was trying to be ironic.

"No," Albert persisted, "that was one of the most difficult things for someone like myself to face. I wasn't alone. It happened to everyone like me who had a little education. It brought us a little way up, but at the same time it put us under. I don't know if this is what was intended."

"So many things built into the job that weren't intended. Didn't get on to it until today that we didn't always see eye to eye."

"I don't think I could have told you that myself then. I shouldn't have told you now. You might not have been so stubborn about going out into the sun."

"I'm going to go ahead with the report," Tony said after a silence. "Can't back out now."

"I never expected you would back out, but I did want to be clear that I wasn't so sure as you about the use of it all."

"I don't know if that's the issue – but I don't have the heart for a debate tonight. We can go back and think about it again when I'm on my feet."

"I shouldn't keep you talking," Albert said, his voice worried. He started to stand up.

"No, please sit," Tony said again, his voice low and strained. They sat without speaking for a few moments. Albert thought he had fallen asleep. He leaned over to look at him. Tony's eyes were open, but he was staring off into space.

"It was good to come back, you know. Imperialism's lackey and all the rest of it. All the things people said about someone like me. I had to see if there was anything in it. I had to see if that's what I'd done with my life."

He clumsily pulled himself to a sitting position, raised his knees and crossed his arms over them.

"But there was more to it. More to it than just that. I think I could have lived with that. But there was this other side to it all. Never spoke to you about it. Never spoke to anyone about it. Just between my wife and myself." He was becoming embarrassed, his voice hanging unsteadily in the flickering light of the stuffy room. "Hardest thing was what it did to Beverly . . . being here. Not just the health part of it. We had enough pills and tablets and bandages to take care of that. She did feel alone sometimes, she didn't know what to do with herself. All the things like this got her down, but they weren't really important. It was the other thing."

He was silent for a moment, then forced himself to go on.

"All of us chaps faced the same problem. What to do about children. Beverly was so keen to have children. When we were talking about getting married that was what she talked about the most. But when you come on station it's not that easy. It isn't so bad the first two or three years if you do go on and have them. Children grow up like weeds out here, everybody's pet. But then comes the time when they have to have schooling. You know, Albert, the school was a good one for a village this size, but it was only for those who were going to stay on in the village. If I'd had children they'd have had to go out into the world. They would have needed every bit of push I could give them, and I didn't know how to go about it.

"A lot of chaps just blundered into it. Didn't give it much thought until it happened. Then they had to decide. Children had to have school, but you didn't want to pack them off to the family in England. You might as well forget you have them. When they're still so young you hate to put them in boarding school. So you saw it happen again and again. Chap's wife went home on leave before he did to see to the children and their school – then stayed on after he was back on station. Then some years she wouldn't get back at all. If they had more than one child that was usually what happened. The poor chap would be stuck out there in the bush thinking about his family all the time and he'd finally pack it in. I know they managed it better on the top – the top fellows could bring in nursemaids and they were down there in the cities where they had a chance at a proper upbringing for their children. But for chaps like me – couldn't make those choices. Had to decide once and for all."

Tony slumped back on the pillow and opened his hands into the dim light, staring at his fingers.

"I didn't let her have children. I couldn't give up the job and I couldn't stand the thought of it here without her; so I said no. And that's what she said to me at the end – you know that, Albert – she said, where are the children. She was off her mind with what they'd given her, but that was what she said, where are the children. And I couldn't answer her."

He stopped talking and covered his eyes with an arm. "Half crazy for a time, losing her."

"Couldn't you have decided any other way to do it? You didn't need to stay on here." Albert was upset with what the other man had told him.

"It seemed simple at the time. Clear about what I was doing and why I had to do it. So I've come back – come back to all this – to see if I did it wrong. Had to come back to the beginning. It's the only thing I could do for her. I'll never know if she forgave me for it, Albert. I don't know if I forgive myself. How do you know when you've got off on the wrong foot – when you hear the marches playing and all the ceremonies and you hear everyone saying that it isn't the wrong foot at all? You just go on marching until you want to drop. And that's what I did."

19.

He slept again. He dreamed.

He dreamed that he was drifting on the river, that he was lying outstretched on its golden sheen. But he had always thought of it as deep green, and he turned his head to see the new color. It was the sun that had turned it to its sudden flaming tone, but the sun hung so close to him that he had to turn his head. As he drifted in the swelling of light the heat hovered so near that he spread his hands over his crotch to shield his body. Now he had no strength in his arms. He was slack and helpless in the stream. Still with his eyes held closed against the sun he felt himself swinging in loose, aimless circles.

When he felt himself touch against something he opened his eyes and found that he was floating at the side of the river steamer and a rope was hanging near him. A little strength had come into his arms and he pulled himself up to the deck. The ship itself wasn't moving, but on either side of it the gleaming current streamed past. He met no one. He saw no one. When he opened the door to their cabin he knew it would be dark inside, and he knew also that if he could grope his way to the bed he would find her in it. When he reached out to put his hands on her he felt again some of his fear. He couldn't touch her. But then he felt her mouth opening to his, and even with the weight of his desperate self-consciousness he found he was embracing her. His hands pressed her naked breasts, her waist, her legs – twisted below them in the sweaty sheet. With his face against hers he could smell her hair, and as he fumbled to hold her closer he realized he was giving way to his tears.

She was whispering to him as he held her. She was whispering ... but then he understood that it wasn't the shadowy figure he held against him who was whispering. He woke to the acrid smell of the mosquito netting, still hearing the whispering, and he lay only a moment hearing it as her voice. When he opened his eyes to the dimness around him, he could pick out the sound of the low voices in the room behind him. He pulled himself up on the pillow, staring heavily around the small, darkened room, but he made no move to lift the curtain. As the sounds of their voices became muffled with the first tentative swaying of Mr. Morrison's trembling bed he drifted back to a half sleep, and in the shadows his wife was beside him again. The two presences merged. They had brought her back to him again. The noise became part of the jumble of sound that hung in the stuffy air around him.

Then he dimly heard sounds of someone walking in the front of the house and he realized Albert was also home. He wondered what time it was, how long he had been sleeping. He couldn't tell from the vague shadows if it was morning or afternoon. He leaned over to find his watch, trying not to make any kind of noise that would interrupt them. He knew from the sounds that for the moment they wouldn't hear him no matter what he did. They seemed less cautious, or he was hearing them more clearly. He could hear her moaning through the grinding heaves of the bed.

He found his watch. It was the middle of the afternoon. Mr. Morrison must have just come home from school.

165

Perhaps this time she had been waiting for him. He leaned back against the pillow, closing his eyes again, when he heard loud footsteps coming up onto the porch in the front of the house. There were voices. Albert was talking with someone. Mr. Smythe leaned out of the bed, straining to hear. He recognized the voice. It was the Commissioner.

For a moment he lay motionless, too dismayed to move. It was all so banal. It was like some kind of vulgar farce. The husband walks in as his wife, in another room, sinks into the arms of another man. Doors fly open, people leap in and out of windows. There is a glimpse of the wife wearing very little, and covering herself with a sheet to suggest that she's wearing even less. There is a great deal of laughter, and when the curtain is lowered the husband – who seems to have deserved it after all – has become reconciled to his situation.

But this wasn't the theater. Tony felt his heart beating in a sluggish protest. He lifted his feet over the edge of the bed, still moving as quietly as possible. He struggled with himself, trying to decide what to do. For a moment his old self, the watchdog of local morals, thought wildly that it was only just that they would be discovered, but he as hurriedly discarded the thought. He had come to feel that somehow what was happening between them was a part of what he had felt for his wife, for Beverly. At the same time he felt sure that what the Commissioner was saying concerned him, and that it was possible he would want to see him.

His heart beating wildly, Tony pushed himself up from the bed, this time trying to make a little noise, enough to interrupt the two in the room behind him. Mr. Jabi and Mr. Camara were speaking loudly in the sitting room. Mr. Morrison and the Commissioner's wife, as he had expected, didn't seem to have heard anything. They were still unconscious of anything except the sounds each of them was making against the other. He debated lifting the curtain for a moment, but he couldn't bring himself to embarrass them. He wouldn't have wanted to be embarrassed himself. He

166

found himself thinking wryly that it would probably be Mr. Morrison who would die of the heart attack. He fumbled for his shorts and his shirt. He knew how he would look, unshaven and his hair tangled, that this would make a poor impression on Camara, but it couldn't be helped. As the voices came closer to his room he finished buttoning his shorts with shaking hands. He forced himself to walk to his door, despite the dizziness that almost overcame him. He pushed the door open, took a step through it, then slammed it behind him, desperately hoping that the sound would finally force its way into the consciousness of the man and the woman behind the window.

He took a step down the short hallway just as Mr. Camara entered it, Mr. Jabi following closely behind him.

"I had no idea you were out of your bed," Mr. Camara said in surprise.

"Just thinking about a little something to eat."

He kept walking and led them away from his own room, into the sitting room.

"Do you think you should be up?" Albert asked. His face was drawn and tight with his concern, though he was trying to smile and hide it.

"You don't look well," Camara said abruptly.

Tony felt himself growing dizzier, but he knew he had to force himself to stay on his feet or they'd take him back to his bed, and the other two wouldn't have a chance to get away. He held out one hand deprecatingly, at the same time holding on to a chair with the other close to his body.

"It's just that I haven't had a chance to shave or comb my hair. Heard your voices and thought I'd come out to see if there was something I could help you with."

"You don't look well. You should sit down." Camara's face was still shining with perspiration and his tight bush shirt showed traces of moisture over his chest and stomach. He was clearly impatient and annoyed.

"If there is a cup of tea ready, a little something to tide me over until supper, I'll sit down and have it here." Tony was

167

trying to sound unconcerned, but he realized that his voice was weakening as he spoke. He slid down into the chair still smiling up at them. With one hand he was trying to push his tangled hair back from his forehead. Albert called to his wife. She came to the doorway and stood silently, staring at Camara, trying not to look toward Smythe. She had heard his voice and she knew that he was too weak to be up. She didn't understand why he had come into the sitting room, but she thought it must have been his last bit of pride. He didn't want the Commissioner to see him lying helpless. She murmured to her husband that she had water ready and she hurried to the kitchen to make tea.

"This is precisely what I have been afraid of ever since you began your visit with us," the Commissioner broke out. He pulled out a chair and sat down opposite Mr. Smythe.

Tony tried to think of a reply. He fumbled for something that would hint at the things he had gathered up to put in his report, but he couldn't collect his thoughts. He stared at the other man, ineffectually trying to roll up his sleeves, trying to think of something to say, as Camara went on.

"I don't want you to feel that you are not welcome with us, but you are not a well man. I learned of your visit to the hospital just after you arrived in the country; so what has happened here to you is nothing new. Am I right? The difficulty is – we have no facilities to care for you."

"Little rest will do it," Tony finally managed to say. He was looking away, his eyes on Mr. Jabi's worried face. He wasn't feeling as dizzy, but it was still difficult for him to concentrate on what he was saying. He was speaking slowly, trying to keep the unsteadiness out of his voice. "Another day or two like this will put me on the mend again. Just seeing to a little work. Things that needed to be done. Should have been a bit more careful getting used to the heat again, but you can't let things sit. A few days rest and I'll be fit."

There was a silence. Camara was studying him, the back of one hand idly tapping against the palm of the other. "This work you have been doing. It can't have been so important

168

for you to run about in the sun at the risk of your health."

"I think that's something I must judge," Tony answered with an effort at being stiffly correct.

"I must say again, it is unfortunate that we have no facilities here to care for someone who is suffering from a serious illness, as you are. I understand it is your heart that is giving you difficulty. I have been in touch with the hospital where you were treated when you first came back to the country. They say that you must have care, and it is the kind of care we can't give you here."

The two men were watching each other carefully, the heavy, sweating, dark Mr. Camara, and the thin, straggling-mustached, sallow Mr. Smythe.

"Just an upset," Mr. Smythe repeated. "Something I'll be over and done with in a day or so."

"You understand you are my responsibility while you are here."

"No I don't understand that."

Mr. Camara stood up impatiently and strode around the room. Mr. Jabi was sitting back in his chair staring down at the floor.

"Come now, Mr. Smythe," Camara said finally, trying to control himself, "Come now. I won't hear of that. You have held this position longer than I have and it must be quite clear to you that everything that goes on here is the responsibility of the Commissioner in one way or another. I am sure you had your nose in everything that went on here, in and out of the village. Isn't that so?"

Tony flinched as Camara turned to him. He was still too weak to hold his thoughts together. He brushed away the question with an uncertain wave of his arm.

"The situation isn't as it was . . ." Mr. Jabi began, trying to interrupt, but when Camara turned toward him he hesitated. "I think Mr. Smythe is not feeling well," he finally added in a mild voice. "I don't think this is the time to discuss his illness."

"Then you'll get him over to see me in the morning, when

169

he's rested." Camara turned again to Mr. Smythe. "I am very sorry that you have been taken sick, but you do understand, I know, that it is only my responsibility to see that something is done for you."

Mr. Camara's intent, angry presence seemed to fill the small, shabby room, and when he went out the door and left them alone the room seemed suddenly empty.

20.

"Mr. Smythe," the Commissioner began, when they met in his office two days later, "As you certainly would be the first to agree with me, this job here that we both have devoted ourselves to is one of considerable difficulty, and it sometimes happens that there is a difficulty, which we could not have foreseen. And even if we had foreseen it we couldn't have resolved it until the difficulty arose. Isn't that so?"

Mr. Smythe was sitting in front of the Commissioner's desk, as before wearing his baggy shorts, his sun helmet on his knees. Mr. Camara was walking about the room, but Tony was making no effort to follow his movements. The Commissioner had put on his khaki uniform for their meeting, but his added weight had come after he'd bought it and the cloth was stretched across his chest and hips. He was already perspiring and he stopped often to wipe his forehead with a handkerchief. The desk had been part of Tony's office furniture for the last three or four years that he'd been on the job. As the Commissioner went on talking Tony slowly reached out and touched the wood, rubbing the grit of dust between his fingers. He was confused as to why

171

Camara had insisted on seeing him, but at the same time he felt at a distance from what was happening, as though he were watching them both from another part of the room.

"I wouldn't, however, have anticipated that there would be a difficulty from the presence of a colleague, and I think I can use that term even if we did not perform our jobs at the same moment of history," Camara continued. It was obvious that he was upset at something, but just as at the evening at his residence he was trying to hide it by becoming long winded and officious. Tony wasn't able to follow what he was saying, so he stared at the maps, at the letter files, turning his head to look – without interest – at the new President of the country. He hadn't heard of the man when he left the service. It must have been one of the younger bunch that none of them knew about.

"So it isn't easy for me. I dislike having to perform duties of this kind, but you would be the first to understand that one cannot turn the other cheek when it is a question of a job to be done."

Mr. Camara went back to his desk, sat down with a sigh and leaned forward, staring into Mr. Smythe's tired face.

"I understood you to say this was a question of my health. Hospital care and the rest of it."

"There are other things which must be discussed as well."

"Then it isn't the hospital you got me over here to talk about."

Camara was abruptly very angry. "I know, of course, what you've been trying to do here," he broke out; then having said it he leaned back in his chair and waited for Mr. Smythe to respond.

"I haven't done anything here," Tony began. Camara interrupted him.

"What about all this investigating you've been doing? All this taking of notes, all this questioning? I have had a dozen people come to me in the last two days asking me what it is you are doing here. You are making yourself free, they tell me."

172

"I think someone has to watch out for them. I'm not doing anything I didn't do before." He was also becoming angry.

"Have you never learned anything? You don't say, in some kind of condescending way to us, 'someone has to watch out for you.' You don't say that in Africa today."

"But I have found . . ." Mr. Smythe found himself unwilling to continue. He couldn't bring himself to begin a discussion with Camara. He looked around the office again and fell silent. As he sat slumped in the chair it seemed to him that the village had also fallen silent. He couldn't remember any other moment when he couldn't hear anything. He turned to look out the door. The mornings had often passed hurriedly for him as he sat in this room working, but always when he lifted his eyes from the desk there had been noises. He turned back and looked at the wall again. The photograph of the country's President was in the same frame that the Queen's picture had been in when he'd had the office. Did they take the frame down and change the picture every time there was a coup, he wondered? Perhaps they had a man who went around and made the appropriate changes, just as the village council in England had sent a man around to check on the light bulbs in the street lamps.

"Smythe," Camara said, after waiting for him to say something, "It has become obvious to me, from the kinds of questions you have been asking, what sort of information you have been looking for. Whatever it is you have found, I believe it could well have been discussed in this office without any kind of irritation to either of us."

Tony was still staring at the wall. Everything that was being said seemed to be coming from somewhere behind him or in another room at a distance. He wondered if his bout of fainting had taken him across some kind of boundary, and whether crossing it had taken him beyond any sort of concern about whatever it was Camara could say to him. He had begun to understand, himself, how his life looked to Camara, and there was no way he could change or alter what the other man felt. He crossed his legs and looked down at his shoes.

"Did you hear what I said?" Camara repeated. "Whatever you think is the issue here could all have been discussed between us. Even when you were in charge of the operation here I am sure there were things which you had to explain to the men who came through from time to time to go over your operation."

Mr. Smythe stood up and went to look at the map that was hanging on the wall. It was the same map that he and Jabi had worked with, and the lines drawn on it seemed to be unchanged. He traced one of the trails with his finger, following it back into the forest, up the scrambling ledges of crumbling red stone he remembered so well. When he'd traveled through that part of his district it had always made him feel that he was in a child's nursery story, trying to climb up the side of a piece of tea cake, and pieces of it came off in his hands as he climbed. The crumbling ledges of red stone had fallen the same way, and the layers of soft rock had given the effect of having been laid there, tentatively, one on top of another, with the intention that whoever came to move the pieces around would do it gently.

"I am trying to talk to you about something," Camara insisted, trying to take control of the situation, but clearly disconcerted by Mr. Smythe's lack of concern. Tony walked back to his chair and sat down again. Just as the Commissioner was about to say something in a louder voice Tony said slowly,

"All the figures I've been looking at in the last day or two make it clear that you've been stealing."

It was Camara's turn to sit without saying anything for a moment. He shrugged. "I knew it was something like that you were pursuing. The questions you were asking would lead only to that. It is unpleasant to hear you say it, even when it isn't true."

"I know what you think of someone like me," Tony said mildly, "but I do know some aspects of the job quite well.

174

You have to, after a time, or you'd never be able to sleep."

"And this tells you I've been stealing?"

"It's all rather obvious. You haven't been very clever about it."

"I still would like to know what you think you've found."

"Oh, let's stop being so pompous about the whole thing. I have found this kind of pilferage in station funds a hundred times. I don't know how anyone thinks they can conceal it. Did you think you would be able to fiddle the books so that no one would notice?"

Camara stared at him without answering. He wiped his forehead with his handkerchief and drummed his fingers on the desk. "I don't know what you're talking about."

Mr. Smythe looked down at his shoes again. He wondered how long Camara wanted to go on talking to him. He listened for a moment and heard the noises outside. They had begun again. He tried to find the familiar threads to weave into the old skein of sound. The dry shaking of palm fronds, the scrabble of chickens beyond the window, a donkey's insistent sobbing.

Camara suddenly lost control of himself, jumped to his feet, slapping his hand down on the desk.

"I won't have this. You have made charges and now you just sit."

"Then you do know what I'm talking about."

"How could I know when you don't say anything," Camara shouted.

"It's the usual thing. Filing vouchers for the purchase of cattle at one price, but paying a lower price and pocketing the difference. Authorizing the payment for top grade materials and accepting the delivery of materials of the lowest grade, if there's delivery at all. And pocketing the difference again. Usually in these cases I found that the supplier was contributing a certain sum which also made its way into your pocket. Sums have been paid for authorized repair work and the repair work hasn't been done. I've been through the vouchers in the allocations section. Your

175

signature is on those vouchers in the allocations section. Your signature is on those vouchers and on the verifications of work completed. You also have signed for the cash all this is supposed to have cost. All the rest of it as well, the usual things. Nothing new."

The Commissioner was standing behind him as he spoke. Mr. Smythe made no effort to turn his head. In his anger Camara stomped to the other side of the room. "You never stop trying to meddle in our affairs. You can never leave us alone. You must always sit there like some judging spirit, looking at us and pointing your finger."

"I haven't done the stealing," Tony answered, shrugging.

"And you think I have?" Camara was still shouting, but he was struggling to get his temper under control.

"I think it's all rather clear. I don't know what else one would have to know."

"But what about explanations, Smythe, clarifications. You could have come to me. It would all have been explained."

Mr. Smythe was silent again. His head was back and he had a thin smile as he watched the other man. With his fingers he was smoothing back his mustache.

The Commissioner walked towards his desk, then abruptly turned and crossed the room and finally sat in a chair against the wall. Tony had the feeling that he was trying to put their conversation on a more personal level by leaving his desk.

"There are, after all, reasons why someone in charge makes the decisions he does, which you know very well. As to the matter of cattle prices, if I have in some cases paid below a certain set sum it was only a matter of trying to make as many purchases as possible to spread income more equitably through the village. As to the materials which you mention, one is often not able to specify quite what one wants and it is a question of making do. And the repairs in question, it is only a matter of time before they are to begin."

Tony suddenly began laughing loudly. "Sorry to be

176

impolite. Do you know, finding a case like this is much less difficult for me now than it was in the old days. I don't have to be so kid gloved about it all. Before it was a matter of making the whole thing go and I had to keep the fellow working with me until I could get someone to take over for him, and I never knew how long that would take. Don't have to give it a thought now. Do you know how many times I've heard those same excuses? When you sat over there and started speaking, I could hear the old wheels turning and I could have given your whole speech myself. If I've seen this kind of theft a hundred times I've heard the same excuses a hundred times. Where are the receipts for the additional cattle purchases? If you signed for first quality materials and received poor quality then you aren't competent to run the show, and you and I know that you never pay for a job until it's completed."

Mr. Camara stood up stiffly. He was so angry that Tony thought for a moment he might strike him. The Commissioner crossed the room and slumped down again behind his desk.

"I didn't ask you here this morning to listen to whatever it is you think you want to say." Camara was perspiring heavily and his shirt was dark with patches of sweat. He wiped his face with an angry gesture. "You don't seem to understand that it is not your role to come here and begin to question, to ferret about. The biggest question is what you did – you and the others like you."

"I didn't steal," Tony remonstrated, still smiling.

"What did you do but steal? It didn't go into your own pocket – you weren't clever enough to take anything for yourself. You kept watch over us while others did the stealing. What is the price of a few cattle or a load of sewer drain pipe compared with the stealing of a country's resources, its customs, its language, its way of life?"

Tony shook his head. "You won't get me into all that. I never put anything into my own pocket, and I don't know of a chap who did."

"I'm talking about the larger issues." Camara was shouting again.

"The ledgers were always up to the minute when I was on station. In twenty years there was never a question about money."

"I must insist that there is a larger question."

"If you can't give a satisfactory answer to this small question, as you put it, then there's no answering the larger one, whatever you think it is." Tony found he was getting tired. He leaned back in the chair and tried to smooth some of the wrinkles out of his shorts.

"You, and the others like you, you were nothing but imperialists." As he said it Camara leaned cross the desk, glaring at Smythe. For him the term had all the pejorative weight that years of speeches by local politicians had given it, and he expected that Smythe would rise to the insult. To his surprise he saw that the term had very little emotional meaning for him. Tony looked away, across the room at the map on the wall.

"The empire simply meant there was a job to be done. Wouldn't have got done otherwise. There was nothing here, Camara. Everything had to be done from the beginning. But no one could say that I took a penny. It wasn't the kind of thing an imperialist like me would do."

"But I would, you are saying. With all your questioning and inferring and so on, you are saying I would do such a thing."

Tony looked at him, shrugged, and looked away. Mr. Camara stood up again and crossed the room. He had become more thoughtful. "I see you don't mind if I call you an imperialist. Then perhaps I should not mind the things you have said about me. They are not true, of course, but you have said them. I can only say that we are all of us only a part of the stream of history. There are larger social forces waiting to be set going. That is the moment which will decide how important it is if the accounts balance or don't balance in this poor place. I can say, however, that history has

178

already made its decision about you and about me. Are you able to understand this? You were a good man here, Smythe, I believe it. I know what has been said about the job you did. You were a good man, but since the job itself was tainted you come to represent its taint. History will say you were a bad man.

"And I, you say? I come at a different moment of history. I am one of the generation who takes over after the imperialists and sets the country going on its own feet and making its way. The accounts ledger will show discrepancies. But history will say that I was a good man. It is only the final decision of history that concerns me."

"I've never heard such nonsense," Tony said, holding up his hands.

"I wasn't sure you had been listening," Camara answered.

They sat for a moment without saying anything. It was difficult to tell if each of them was thinking about what the other had said — or if they had simply forgotten about each other. Tony was also feeling the heat in the small room. When he had worked at the desk he had usually had a boy to work the fan if he had to deal with petitioners. He looked toward the closed window, but he knew that opening it didn't help until later in the afternoon when the sun had dropped down behind the trees. He had never been able to make any progress with the sun. For twenty years its swelling ball of heat had kept him as helpless as he had been during his first weeks on the post. Now his legs were pale from his English winters, but he could already see the irritated redness where the sun had burned his bare knees.

Camara finally stood up and stood in the center of the room, one hand behind his back.

"It has been a most interesting discussion, Smythe, and what you have said does make it clear that your intention has been to stir up a situation that does not concern you. What I asked you here for was rather painful for me, but as one must do one's duty – as you would be the first to agree – I find that the things you have said will make it less painful for me. You have come into the country on a visa which specifies that what you will be doing here is tourism. Your activities have stepped over the limit of friendly tourism, so I have requested that your visa be withdrawn. You will leave the district as soon as you have got your things together and you can arrange for transportation. To cause less confusion I am saying that it is for reasons of health. I cannot take responsibility for you here, and you can return to hospital when you've gone back to the coast."

Tony sat back in the chair, his eyes closed. "You can't simply put someone out."

"Why not?"

"Such a long way to get here. Friends and all that."

"You should have kept these things in mind."

Tony was conscious of a distance to everything that was happening in the room, but at the same time he felt a kind of helplessness, and he tried to force it to one side with an abrupt gesture. "But you can't do this," he said again.

"It isn't a question of whether or not I can do it. I think to avoid excitement in the district, I have no other choice. Wouldn't you have done the same thing if someone had come along while you were here and had begun building up some sort of case against what you'd been doing? Wouldn't you have brought him into this office and said to him just what I'm saying to you?"

Tony looked up into his dark, sweating face. "You know I have all the materials I need for the report I'm going to make. Only a question of putting it together. After that I don't see what all of this rigmarole you're talking about will have to do with anything."

Camara began to laugh, and he went to the chair against the wall and sat down again, still laughing. "Mr. Smythe, I have never talked at length with someone who had held a post like this in the colonial period, and I must say I find you a little surprising. You would never make a politician, since

180

you seem to know nothing of strengths and weaknesses and I'm afraid that's all one has to build a career on. My wife's father is one of the ministers responsible for the development of areas such as this and the purchasing and supplying you have questioned are in his hands. He is taking a keen interest in my career. Whatever report you have to make about the situation here will have to come to his hands first, and he will take the matter up with me. He may question some of my decisions, but I'm sure I'll be able to explain anything he is doubtful of."

"So you can just toss me out."

"Yes, I can."

Mr. Smythe sat without speaking. It had grown so hot in the room he was beginning to sweat as much as Mr. Camara. He found, now that it was all out, that what he'd been doing didn't seem to be that important to him. For him the most important thing had been to feel for a moment that he was doing something again. It had been like that when he was on post. It was doing the job that mattered. He had never worried himself about how it would all come out. He would think about leaving later. He was still too weak to travel in the heat for a few days at least, and he knew that Camara wouldn't hurry him, as long as he stayed close to Jabi and asked no more questions.

With a shrug he looked across the room at the Commissioner. "I understand a great deal of what you're saying, Camara. I'm not the fool you obviously think I am. I have thought about some of this." He broke off and looked down at his stained sun helmet, still sitting in his lap. He ran a finger around the rim, then looked again at the map on the wall. "Our thoughts on it – yours and mine – don't seem to be on the same planet. How could they be, Camara? You grew up in the days when we were still here – you could see what we were trying to do, what we were trying to build. How could you see it all in such a different way?"

"Smythe – Smythe, what to do with you!" The Commissioner began laughing; then suddenly his voice

181

hardened. "I am not one of those village elders who can draw from his tradition some wise saying that gives us a clear insight into any question. Perhaps I can make one up which would describe how it is that you as the white man coming to this place, and I who am part of this place could see what you did in such a different light. What I can tell you is that the lion and the antelope are both present at the death of the antelope, but the antelope's view of what is happening is certainly different from the lion's."

21.

He had sat so many times in the shadow of the porch and watched the evening settle over the village. Tony had brought out a chair and was sitting alone looking out beyond the compound fence to the ragged forms of the palm fronds as they leaned their weight down toward the bent trunks. Birds were circling the trees, solitary swallows pursuing insects, flocks of small field birds settling onto spiny branches with a convulsive spate of chattering and fluttering. Albert was still away from the house. He had gone to try to persuade the Commissioner to change his mind. Tony didn't think he would be successful. He found that it didn't seem important to him, he only wanted to have more time. He wanted to spend more days in the village, days when he did nothing except feel the shifts of light and heat and haze and dust. The light in the tops of the trees had turned to a rich amber. It would soon be sunset. He thought for a moment of making himself a drink. He'd brought something with him. It was still in his suitcase. He decided against it. He would have to go back to his room to get his suitcase, and if he went back to his room he'd probably want to nap again.

He preferred to stay outside and watch the sky darken.

He had been sitting almost an hour when someone came into the yard through the gate. Surprised, he saw that it was the Commissioner's wife. At the same moment he remembered the last time he had seen her, and to cover his rush of embarrassment he tried to get to his feet. He was unsteady and the chair fell back against the wall behind him. She watched uncomfortably as he fumbled to get it back on its legs again.

"I didn't mean to make you get up." She was as nervous and self-conscious as the first time he'd seen her.

"No. Don't give it a thought. Just didn't see who it was when you first turned in the gate."

"But you mustn't stand up. I've just been listening to Mr. Jabi and my husband discuss your illness."

"I'm sure they have nothing good to say, but I will sit. Can you get a chair in there? I'd get it myself, but if you've heard them talking I'm sure you've heard them say I mustn't do anything."

Still uncomfortable with him she slipped into the door to the sitting room and came out with another chair that she put on the other side of the porch. They sat looking at each other. Looking again at her carefully fitted clothes, at her slim body and legs, he tried to reconcile the two images he had of her, the woman hungrily embracing Mr. Morrison in the darkened room, and the earnest, ill-at-ease Commissioner's wife sitting at a distance from him in the lengthening shadows. As he had found before, the conflicting impressions were so difficult to assemble into a single figure.

"Do you think they'll send me off?" he asked her after a pause.

"I don't think there's any question that something has to be done. The little medical station that was here – that isn't even working any more. What can we do with you?"

"I don't know. No one could ever do much. Do you know you're still shy with me?" he said suddenly.

"I don't think I am, Mr. Smythe," she said with her voice

184

earnest, but he could hear a slight tremor as she spoke.

"No matter. Do you know no one has ever told me your name, except Mrs. Camara, which seems too formal for the two of us when we're sitting on the porch watching the sun go down."

"Ruth. My name is Ruth."

"It's not an African name."

"My father's in the government and he wanted us to have European names. I have an African name as well, but it is very long and very difficult to pronounce."

"I'm Tony."

"I don't think . . . I couldn't ever call you that."

"Because I'm so difficult?" he laughed.

"No. Because you've always been Mr. Smythe." She was becoming a little more relaxed, but she was still sitting with her hands clenched in her lap.

"My wife – her name was Beverly – was always shy when she met someone new here. I would have thought she'd get over it, but we had so few visitors she got just as nervous each time someone new showed up. Didn't matter if it was a chap who had gone to school with me. She used to try and learn as much about each new chap as she could – making it easier for him was her way of putting it. 'We'll have that much more to talk about.' But it was only for herself." He sat staring into the trees. "She was very lonely here." His voice was lower, softer. "I didn't know then how lonely she was. She didn't think it was important to tell me about. What about you?"

"Why . . . I mean how could I be lonely when I have things to do . . . in the village. I am a part of my husband's job," she finished lamely.

"Beverly said the same thing. At least I think she would have, if I'd asked her. What about children – Ruth – is it Ruth? What about children?"

"I think about them. I do."

"But you haven't thought of when you might have them?"

"I still have to travel so much to be with my husband. It

185

seems so necessary just now. But it will come in time. A family nowadays can come in time, isn't that so?" She tried to end on a light tone.

"Do it now." His tone was so serious that she stared at him in surprise. He looked away. "Didn't mean to sound so determined about it all. Just don't let the chance go by, you mustn't."

There was a slow, langorous atmosphere around the village. Voices were low, the laughter of the children seemed almost thoughtful. The light had flamed up into an orange crescent that burned through the woven matting of the trees. He watched it without speaking, almost forgetting she was still with him.

"What did she do while she was here?" The woman's voice was low, still diffident and self-conscious.

"Do?"

"I am speaking about your wife. What did she do with her time when she was here?"

"Always had something waiting for her. On the go every minute. She took to the life here. Took to the people. Always in the village looking after somebody. She wanted to be right with me, doing the job together. I think that's what made it possible for us to stay on. Most wives didn't have such a keen interest. But Beverly gave it everything. Don't think she regretted a day of it."

He was speaking with such assurance that she didn't know how to answer him. "But she was lonely, you said."

"Yes," he said, his voice again low and soft. "Yes, she was lonely."

A few minutes later Mrs. Camara stood up awkwardly and said she had to leave. She had only come by to see how he was feeling, she had told her husband she would be back when she'd seen Mr. Smythe.

"But you'll come back again?" Tony had got to his feet again and had taken her hand.

186

"I don't know how long you'll be here."

He shrugged. "As your husband said I'm not well at all. I'm not well enough to go anywhere for the moment. Wouldn't do at all until I've got my strength back a bit." He dropped her hand. "But do come. I'd like to tell you about Beverly. I'd like to tell you about her and the things she did while she was here. It was almost twenty years, you know. The best part of her life."

Mrs. Camara went toward the steps, but she smiled at him suddenly. Her expression was shy, but he felt for the first time that she had begun to understand him. "I will try to come again, if I don't have too much to do. And if you are still here." And she turned and hurried across the yard.

He stood in the shadows watching her leave. He could feel the heat again. Would be pleasant if she came another time. He picked up the chairs and carried them into the sitting room, then he went into Mr. Jabi's study and sat down to wait until he came back. There were so many things he had remembered he wanted to tell him about. He stared out of the window into the shadows that had begun to etch deep lines into the fronds of the palm trees beyond the compound fence. Would he have time to tell him all the things he wanted? He thought about it as the room slowly darkened.

22.

Some weeks later Mr. Camara was given temporary leave from his duties as District Commissioner to attend a conference on new policies to develop a political consciousness in the African countryside. The conference was to be held in a city to the south, and he was scheduled to take an afternoon flight from the airport on the coast. A government car took him out to the one room airport building and, as usual, he was thinking about the speech he had been asked to make as the car clattered over the poorly paved road to the terminal that lay fifteen miles outside the small capital city. His wife had come as far as the coast with him, but while he was away she preferred to spend a few days with her family. With a self-conscious shift of his shoulders, settling himself deeper into the back seat of the car, he told himself that she'd already been to so many conferences, it wasn't necessary for her to follow along to this one as well.

Since the capital city was still small the road followed the old meandering stretch of a path that had been built close to the beach by the first British governors. The road began at the clump of buildings that had served as residence and seat of government for the British colony, and as it trailed beside the elongated stretch of beach leading out of the city it passed most of the other buildings that had housed the local government. Beyond the town, on a stretch of dessicated earth just above the sandy strip of beach, it passed the cemetery. Most of the newer graves were Moslem, and the writing on the markers was in Arabic, but close to the road was an older section that still had some of the feeling of a Victorian church cemetery. It was overgrown with thorn bushes and the stucco was peeling from the sides of the crypts but there was an atmosphere of pervasive calm among the carved headstones and stucco angels – even with the rasp of African birds calling through the thorn branches and the sun flooding over all of it with its withering glare.

Camara had driven the road to the airport so many times that he hardly bothered to look out the window of the car, and he didn't notice the small group in the old section of the cemetery. Mr. Jabi looked up as the car passed, but he didn't see the Commissioner, only the dark shape of the car as it lurched past them on the rutted road. Tony had left no instructions as to what Mr. Jabi should do with his body, and at first he had thought that they should bury him in the village, but the cemetery was badly maintained and Mr. Smythe would be the only European buried there. After much discussion he had made arrangements for Tony to be buried on the coast. Tony had known some of the others who were already buried there. It was a hot day and the humid air blowing in from the sea felt heavy and sticky after the drier air of their village. Mr. Jabi and the others who had come with him for the funeral were in their best suits, and they were feeling the effects of the heat. Suso was fanning himself with his hat as he stood with his head bowed, listening to the prayers. Mr. Jabi was crying, though he had his head turned away from the others so they wouldn't see his streaked face.

There were flowers at the graveside, a few wreaths lying against the heap of dry earth that had been scratched out of the hard beach ground. There had been a little money with Tony's things, however, and Albert had arranged for a head stone that would be placed on the grave when it was finished. There had been a great deal of discussion in his sitting room as to what the head stone should say. Most of the men who had come to greet Mr. Smythe on his return had stopped by to offer their suggestions. Finally they had all settled on a simple epitaph that Mr. Jabi had presented for consideration. Following Tony Smythe's name it was to say "Beloved of his wife and mourned by all who knew him." There had been considerable argument about a final line, but at the end they had all agreed that under this would be written, "A Friend to his Country."